The Cupcake Diaries:
Sweet On You

Also by Darlene Panzera

Bet You'll Marry Me

Coming Soon
The Cupcake Diaries: Recipe for Love
The Cupcake Diaries: Taste of Romance

THE CUPCAKE DIARIES
Sweet On You

DARLENE PANZERA

AVONIMPULSE
An Imprint of HarperCollinsPublishers

Excerpt from *The Cupcake Diaries: Recipe for Love* copyright © 2013 by Darlene Panzera.

Excerpt from *The Cupcake Diaries: Taste of Romance* copyright © 2013 by Darlene Panzera.

Excerpt from *Stealing Home* copyright © 2013 by Candice Wakoff.

Excerpt from *Lucky Like Us* copyright © 2013 by Jennifer Ryan.

Excerpt from *Stuck On You* copyright © 2013 by Cheryl Harper.

Excerpt from *The Right Bride* copyright © 2013 by Jennifer Ryan.

Excerpt from *Lachlan's Bride* copyright © 2013 by Kathleen Harrington.

EPub Edition MAY 2013 ISBN: 9780062242662

Print Edition ISBN: 9780062242679

JV 10 9 8 7 6 5 4

For my children,
Samantha, Robert, and Jason
And in loving memory of
Denise Bova Gant
February 11, 1979–March 25, 2012

Chapter One

Forget love . . . I'd rather fall in chocolate!
—Author unknown

ANDI CAST A glance over the rowdy karaoke crowd to the man sitting at the front table with the clear plastic bakery box in his possession.

"What am I supposed to say?" she whispered, looking back at her sister, Kim, and their friend Rachel as the three of them huddled together. "Can I have your cupcake? He'll think I'm a lunatic."

"Say 'please,' and tell him about our tradition," Kim suggested.

"Offer him money." Rachel dug through her dilapidated Gucci knockoff purse and withdrew a ten-dollar bill. "And let him know we're celebrating your sister's birthday."

"You did promise me a cupcake for my birthday," Kim said with an impish grin. "Besides, the guy doesn't look like he plans to eat it. He hasn't even glanced at the cupcake since the old woman came in and delivered the box."

Andi tucked a loose strand of her dark blond hair behind her ear and drew in a deep breath. She wasn't used to taking food from anyone. Usually she was on the other end—giving it away. Her fault. She didn't plan ahead.

Why couldn't any of the businesses here be open twenty-four hours like in Portland? Out of the two dozen eclectic cafes and restaurants along the Astoria waterfront promising to satisfy customers' palates, shouldn't at least one cater to late-night customers like herself? No, they all shut down at 10:30, some earlier, as if they knew she was coming. That's what she got for living in a small town. Anticipation but no cake.

However, she was determined not to let her younger sister down. She'd promised Kim a cupcake for her twenty-sixth birthday, and she'd try her best to procure one, even if it meant making a fool of herself.

Andi shot her ever-popular friend Rachel a wry look. "You know you're better at this than I am."

Rachel grinned. "You're going to have to start interacting with the opposite sex again sometime."

Maybe. But not on the personal level, Rachel's tone suggested. Andi's divorce the previous year had left behind a bitter aftertaste no amount of sweet talk could dissolve.

Pushing back her chair, she stood up. "Tonight, all I want is the cupcake."

ANDI HAD TAKEN only a few steps when the man with the bakery box turned his head and smiled.

He probably thought she was coming over, hoping to find a date. Why shouldn't he? The Captain's Port was filled with people looking for a connection, if not for a lifetime, then at least for the hour or so they shared within the friendly confines of the restaurant's casual, communal atmosphere.

She hesitated midstep before continuing forward. Heat rushed into her cheeks. Dressed in jeans and a navy blue tie and sport jacket, he was even better looking than she'd first thought. Thirtyish. Light brown hair, fair skin with an evening shadow along his jaw, and the most amazing gold-flecked, chocolate brown eyes she'd ever seen. *Oh my.* He could have his pick of any woman in the place. Any woman in Astoria, Oregon.

"Hi," he said.

Andi swallowed the nervous tension gathering at the back of her throat and managed a smile in return. "Hi. I'm sorry to bother you, but it's my sister's birthday, and I promised her a cupcake." She nodded toward the see-through box and waved the ten-dollar bill. "Is there any chance I can persuade you to sell the one you have here?"

His brows shot up. "You want my cupcake?"

"I meant to bake a batch this afternoon," she gushed, her words tumbling over themselves, "but I ended up packing spring break lunches for the needy kids in the school district. Have you heard of the Kids' Coalition backpack program?"

He nodded. "Yes, I think the *Astoria Sun* featured the free lunch backpack program on the community page a few weeks ago."

"I'm a volunteer," she explained. "And after I finished, I tried to buy a cupcake but didn't get to the store in time. I've never let my sister down before, and I feel awful."

The new addition to her list of top ten dream-worthy males leaned back in his chair and pressed his lips together, as if considering her request, then shook his head. "I'd love to help you, but—"

"*Please.*" Andi gasped, appalled she'd stooped to begging. She straightened her shoulders and lifted her chin. "I understand if you can't, it's just that my sister, Kim, my friend Rachel, and I have a tradition."

"What kind of tradition?"

Andi pointed to their table, and Kim and Rachel smiled and waved. "Our birthdays are spaced four months apart, so we split a celebration cupcake three ways and set new goals for ourselves from one person's birthday to the next. It's easier than trying to set goals for an entire year."

"I don't suppose you could set your goals without the cupcake?" he asked, his eyes sparkling with amusement.

Andi smiled. "It wouldn't be the same."

"If the cupcake were mine to give, it would be yours. But this particular cupcake was delivered for a research project I have at work."

"Wish I had your job." Andi dropped into the chair he pulled out for her and placed her hands flat on the table. "What if I told you it's been a really tough day, tough week, tough year?"

He pushed his empty coffee cup aside, and the corners of his mouth twitched upward. "I'd say I could argue the same."

"But did you spend the last three hours running all over town looking for a cupcake?" she challenged, playfully mimicking Rachel's flirtatious, sing-song tone. "The Pig 'n Pancake was closed, along with the supermarket, and the cafe down the street said they don't even sell them anymore. And then . . . I met you."

He covered her left hand with his own, and although the unexpected contact made her jump, she ignored the impulse to pull her fingers away. His gesture seemed more an act of compassion than anything else, and, frankly, she liked the feel of his firm yet gentle touch.

"What if I told you," he said, leaning forward, "that I've traveled five hundred and seventy miles and waited sixty-three days to taste this one cupcake?"

Andi leaned toward him as well. "I'd say that's ridiculous. There's no cupcake in Astoria worth all that trouble."

"What if this particular cupcake isn't from Astoria?"

"No?" She took another look at the box but didn't see a label. "Where's it from?"

"Hollande's French Pastry Parlor outside of Portland."

"What if I told you I would send you a dozen Hollande's cupcakes tomorrow?"

"What if I told *you*," he said, and stopped to release a deep, throaty chuckle, "this is the last morsel of food I have to eat before I starve to death today?"

Andi laughed. "I'd say that's a good way to go. Or I could invite you to my place and cook you dinner."

Her heart stopped, stunned by her own words, then rebooted a moment later when their gazes locked, and he smiled at her.

"You can have the cupcake on one condition."

"Which is?"

Giving her a wink, he slid the bakery box toward her. Then he leaned his head in close and whispered in her ear.

Chapter Two

> There is nothing better than a friend, unless it is a
> friend with chocolate.
>
> —Charles Dickens

ELATED, ANDI RETURNED to Rachel and Kim with the
prize in hand—or at least three-fourths of the prize. She
set the gourmet chocolate cupcake topped with white
icing and crushed toffee candy sprinkles on the table in
front of them.

"You got it!" Rachel squealed. "Did you get his phone
number, too?"

Andi flushed. She didn't even get his name. After
he smiled at her that second time, all she could do
was stare at him like a gaping idiot. "No, just the cupcake."

"Why is there a piece missing?" Kim pointed. "Did he bite into it before you got there?"

"No," she said, unable to stop grinning. "He said instead of splitting the cupcake three ways, we'd have to cut it in four."

Rachel bobbed her curly head. "Fair enough."

Kim helped Andi divvy up the three remaining cupcake pieces onto paper napkins, and without being asked, their waitress brought over a candle and a pack of matches.

"Compliments from the man up front," the waitress told them.

Andi turned around to give him an appreciative nod, and he smiled a third time.

"Somebody's in trouble," Rachel sang getting up from her seat.

Andi frowned. She wasn't in trouble. For once in her life, she'd accomplished what she'd set out to do: she got the cupcake.

"Oh, no," Kim moaned.

Andi followed her sister's fearful gaze toward Rachel, who had walked over to the karaoke singer with the microphone. The sound system crackled twice.

Then the male singer, whose belly strained against his red suspenders, cleared his throat and announced, "I hear we have someone celebrating her birthday tonight." He pointed at Kim, who looked as if she wanted to crawl under the table to hide. "Everyone sing 'Happy Birthday' to Kimberly Nicole Burke."

Andi lit the candle on the cupcake, and after the song,

Kim blew out the flame to the applause of everyone in the room.

"I'm surprised you didn't take the microphone out of his hands and perform your sultry nightclub rendition," Andi teased when Rachel returned to her seat.

"I don't sing in public," Rachel said, tossing her red curls over her shoulder. "It might ruin my image."

"You're wrong," Andi said, distributing the remaining three bite-sized pieces of the sweet, perfectly iced, dreamy-gooey, chocolate lovers' cupcake. "I think your voice is beautiful."

Rachel grinned. "That's what friends are for."

Andi turned to her sister. "Did you make a wish?"

"I wished for a job, so I can get my own apartment instead of living at home with Dad."

Andi's heart went out to her. "You didn't get the position at the art gallery?"

Kim's delicate dark brows drew together as she shook her head. "No. They gave it to someone else. How about you?"

"There are only so many dentists in Astoria, and the offices I visited aren't hiring any dental assistants right now. It doesn't help that I haven't worked since before Mia was born, and I'm not familiar with the new technology."

Kim leaned forward, her face solemn. "Any word on your deadbeat ex?"

Andi shook her head. "No. He's still missing, and the authorities can't find him. He hasn't paid child support in over four months, and the money I've spent on lawyers and PIs trying to track him down has put me in more debt than the divorce. As of today, I'm a full month behind with my rent."

Rachel glanced down at the table. "I'm afraid I can't help. I got fired two weeks ago."

Andi gasped. "Why didn't you tell me?"

"I don't know. Too embarrassed maybe? My boss said I spent too much time talking and not enough time taking orders."

"You were the best coffee barista he had," Andi said, clenching her fists. "How dare he fire you after all you've done for him!"

Rachel lifted her head. "You're right."

"You didn't like working there anyway," Kim added.

"Right again," Rachel agreed. "I wish I could run my own business where I could be my own boss and not have anyone tell me what to do. My ex-boss *lives* to order other people around. All the baristas call him the 'Bossina-tor.' He complained I was never early enough, never fast enough, never good enough no matter what I did."

Andi nodded. "He sounds like my father."

"Worse." Rachel sighed. "I won't be moving out of my room over the garage any time soon. But at least I have my own entrance, and my mom doesn't care if I can't pay the rent on time. I'd invite you to move in with me—except there isn't space for any more people now that my grandpa Lewy has come to stay."

"I know." Andi thought of her five-year-old daughter, Mia, and wondered how she would continue to support her on her own.

Then her gaze shifted to the cupcake. Hallelujah for chocolate to lighten the mood when the weight of the world grew too heavy!

Split three ways, four this time, the cupcake was less fattening. Also, less guilt afterward. Picking up her share, Andi popped the bite-sized piece into her mouth and closed her eyes, waiting to be transported to heaven.

What she got was the opposite. Chewing slowly, she glanced about for a glass of water. Not seeing any, she motioned for the waitress and then brushed the crumbs that had fallen from her fingers off her shirt.

"Dry," she said, trying to push the remainder of the wretched icing past her tongue.

"Eck." Rachel scrunched her face in disgust. "I thought the cupcake was the best thing we had going tonight, but the chocolate didn't even taste like chocolate."

Kim wiped her mouth with her napkin. "Reminds me of cow dung."

"This cupcake reminds me of men," Rachel said, lifting her chin. "Sweet, good-looking, and promising when you first meet. Then dry, messy, and disappointing once you get into the relationship."

"They shouldn't be disappointing," Kim declared.

Andi laughed. "Are you talking about cupcakes or men?"

"Both."

Rachel stuck out her tongue. "Andi, you bake better cupcakes than this."

"I've had lots of practice. I used to bake with Mom, and now I make cupcakes with Mia for birthday parties at school."

"We should open a cupcake shop!" Rachel's face lit up and she clapped her hands together. "You can teach us how to bake, and then we'd never have to eat another disappointing cupcake again!"

"We'd end up eating them all," Andi said, imagining her waistline expanding like a balloon. "And I'm already ten pounds more than my ideal weight."

"None of us have jobs, we all need money, and we love cupcakes, Kim said, counting off the facts on her fingers. "Opening a cupcake shop is the perfect solution."

"It would be fun," Rachel agreed. "Exciting. And it's something we could do together."

Andi rolled her eyes. "I can't even pay my rent. How could I start up a small business?"

"We could apply for a bank loan," Kim offered.

"Astoria doesn't have a good gourmet cupcake shop," Rachel pointed out, her tone transforming into a lyrical theatrical performance. "Four months ago on my birthday, we agreed to take charge and change our lives, but nothing changed. If we open a cupcake shop, we could change *everything*."

"Yes, we could change the world with cupcakes." Andi grinned. "I've always dreamed of opening a bakery. Imagine us, running a cupcake shop."

"I could decorate the cakes," Kim added, "make them look like gourmet treats too fancy to pass up."

"You could decorate the walls with your paintings, too, like your own art gallery," Andi encouraged.

"And we could make different flavors, like black cherry cheesecake, vanilla-hazelnut, and strawberry lemonade,"

Rachel continued, as if talking to herself. "I could be the spokesperson and go on TV and tell everyone about our famous gourmet cupcakes. Imagine crowds of people lined up at the door. And I know how to shop."

"How would that help?" Andi asked.

Rachel's rosy cheeks glowed through the thick layer of foundation she used to hide her freckles. "I could spot deals on supplies, color coordinate the interior, and decorate window displays to draw people through the door."

"And you could flirt with all the men," Andi teased.

"Of course!" Rachel laughed. "I would hope there would be some men. Can you imagine me in a little pink frilly apron, serving cupcakes and hosting parties—lots of parties?"

"Instead of a coffee barista, you could be a cupcake barista," Andi said, playing along. "And we could call the shop Captivated by Cupcakes or Cupcake Obsession."

"Andi's Private Stash," Kim supplied. "Or maybe The Cupcake Connoisseur."

Andi looked back at the cupcake guy, smiled, and said, "Simply Irresistible."

"How about Cupcake Connection?" Rachel suggested. "A shop that brings people together over cupcakes. It worked for Andi. Her cupcake man keeps glancing in her direction every five seconds."

Andi shot him a second look and gasped, realizing Rachel was right. "Cupcakes R Us."

"Ooh!" Rachel pounded the table with her fist. "We

can be 'Cupcake Chicks' or 'The Cupcake Crew' and call the shop Keep 'em Coming Cupcakes."

"It's taking the waitress a long time to come back over here," Andi said with a frown.

Kim snapped her fingers. "How about The Perfect Cupcake?"

"No, not that one," Andi said, shaking her head. "We aren't perfect. Better to say we're creative rather than perfect. Creative is a better reflection of us and our product. Creative Cupcakes."

The waitress arrived, apologized for the delay, and set three water glasses on the table.

Rachel caught her eye. "What do you think about a trio of women with no business experience opening a cupcake shop?"

The waitress smiled. "The owner of this place didn't know anything about business when he started. He had friends help out and make sure he did everything right. Must have worked. The Captain's Port is a success."

Rachel shrugged. "Well, if he did it, so can we. This can be our new goal until Andi's birthday in July. And when we make the shop a success, we'll buy ourselves a big, fancy, gold-plated cake cutter."

"Yeah, a knife as big as a short sword to hang on the wall of the shop for everyone to see," Andi joked.

Kim agreed. "We can use it every four months on each of our birthdays to cut the cake."

"What's stopping us?" Rachel asked.

Andi laughed so hard tears formed in her eyes. "Maybe a heavy dose of reality?"

"Get ready for this reality," Rachel warned. "'Simply Irresistible' is headed your way."

Andi turned her head, and the cupcake guy walked up to their table.

"So, how was it?" he asked.

Andi couldn't stop looking at him. "Thank you, it was . . . good."

"Would have been great with milk," Rachel added.

"I wish I'd had a fork to pick up every last morsel," Kim said, failing to keep a straight face.

The cupcake guy laughed, and Andi laughed with him from sheer giddiness due to his close proximity.

"Meaning," he said, giving them each a direct look, "you are trying to be polite, but the cupcake was horribly bland, dry, and crumbly. Hmm. I thought so, too. Thanks, ladies."

Andi gushed, "We really did appreciate it, uh—"

"Jake. Jake Hartman." He took a business card out of his pocket and placed it on the table. "If you're ever in dire need of a cupcake again, give me a call."

Andi wasn't sure, but she thought his gaze lingered on her a few seconds longer than on Rachel and Kim. Or maybe it was just her heart beating twice as fast. In the end, it didn't matter, because he turned without another word and walked out the door.

"Did you see the way he looked at you?" Rachel crooned.

Andi grunted. "He must think we're idiots."

"Jake works for the local paper." Kim picked up his card. "The *Astoria Sun*. And he left you his phone number."

"Yeah," Andi said, her voice catching in her throat, "but he didn't ask for mine."

Rachel elbowed her. "He gave you his number; maybe he was waiting for you to give him yours."

"Do you think?" Hope sprang from the well where it had been hiding, but Andi stuffed the emotion back down where it belonged. "Well, then I just blew it."

"You didn't want a date anyway," Kim reminded her.

"Right," Andi agreed. She looked toward the front door. "All I wanted was the cupcake."

WHEN ANDI GOT home at 11:30, her seventeen-year-old babysitter met her at the door.

"I tried," Heather insisted, "but Mia wouldn't go to sleep."

"Mommy!" Mia pushed past Heather and ran outside to hug her legs.

Andi bent to give Mia a hug, then handed Heather a twenty and watched the teenager slip into the house next door.

The night was dark, and a thick layer of mist had rolled in from the water. A foghorn's long, drawn out wail sounded in the distance, warning the boats away from the unseen shore. Andi was about to make her way safely back into her own house when a man jumped from the shadows and drew near.

Her first reaction was to wrap her arms protectively around her daughter. The second was to scream.

The man, who wore a perfect camouflage of matching

gray pants and jacket, asked, "Are you Andrea Leanne Burke?" He held a manila envelope in his hands.

"Yes," she answered, taking the envelope from him.

Could it be some legal document pertaining to her ex-husband's financial responsibility? Had the PI found him? Would she get money from him to pay her rent?

The man in gray disappeared as quickly as he'd come, and she tore open the envelope, anxious to see what news awaited her. At the top of the paper inside, written in bold black lettering, was the title EVICTION NOTICE.

Andi sucked in her breath and her stomach knotted up tight. If she didn't bring her rent current by the end of the month, they'd have to find a new place to live. She'd suspected this might happen. That's why she hadn't invited Kim or Rachel to move in.

Beside her, Mia's small voice broke into her thoughts. "What's that, Mommy?"

"Nothing." She crumbled the paper in her hand, ushered Mia into the house, and glanced around at all the items she might not be able to keep. "Let's get your pajamas on and get ready for bed."

"I already have my pajamas on."

Andi focused on her daughter's attire. Mia was wearing her favorite pink bunny print pajamas reminding her that the last day of the month was also Easter, a holiday she usually anticipated with joy.

"Mommy, will we have to move again?"

"Move? I hope not," Andi said, trying to keep her tone light. "Where did you hear that?"

"Grandpa." Mia looked up at her with big blue eyes.

"He says you have no money, and we'll have to move in with him and have my birthday party there."

Andi stiffened. How dare her father discuss her financial situation with her child! He didn't know anything about her finances. No, her father made his own assumptions, usually negative, and accepted them as truth.

Worse, most of the time her father was right.

She had always wanted a place with a water view and didn't want to leave, nor did she want to move Mia again. Her daughter had dealt with enough change. They both had. What they needed most was a stable home.

After her divorce settlement, she'd rented this adorable cottage on the hillside for her and Mia. Andi loved the front porch best because it faced the wide mouth of the Columbia River. She could see the lights on the big cargo ships as they passed by at night, traveling west toward the Pacific Ocean. She could draw the calming, seawater air into her lungs. And she could hear the languid calls of the circling gulls, which eased her stress after a hard day. No wonder Astoria was the oldest American settlement west of the Rockies. Who wouldn't want to live here?

Andi swallowed hard. She had thirty days to pay her rent, or she'd have to take Mia and move back in with her condescending father, who had always suggested she couldn't make it on her own. Not a pleasant thought. Instead she recalled what Rachel and Kim had said at the Captain's Port, and her brain began to churn with ideas.

"I'll get the money," she vowed. "Because I'm going to open a cupcake shop." She glanced down at Mia. "You like cupcakes, right?"

Mia nodded her little blond head.

"That's why it will be a success." Andi hugged her daughter close. "Who doesn't love cupcakes?"

Chapter Three

Business Plan: Get loan. Apply for permits. Find
storefront shop. Buy equipment. Advertise. Bake.
Sell. Pay rent.

THE FOLLOWING MORNING Andi met Rachel and Kim in
the bank lobby with a note binder and a plate of chocolate
truffle cupcakes topped with ganache and cocoa powder.

"When did you have time to bake?" Rachel demanded,
her eyes wide.

Andi shrugged. "I stayed up all night."

"That would explain the insane phone call I received
from you this morning."

"This is not insane. We can do this."

"I never expected you to take me seriously," Rachel
whispered as they approached the financing desk.

Andi looked from Rachel to Kim. "Why shouldn't

we open a cupcake company? If no one will hire us, we'll create our own jobs. We'll be entrepreneurs. Did you know that the first chocolate cake was baked in the year 1674?"

"I see you did your research, but we'll need a shop," Rachel persisted.

"Yes, and in the meantime we can rent an approved kitchen and bake our cupcakes there. I downloaded an application for a small business license from the internet and as soon as we get a bank loan for supplies and start taking orders—we'll be in business. We can also sell cupcakes at fairs, festivals, and the Farmer's Market." Andi frowned at her sister. "Kim, you haven't said a word. What do you think?"

Kim's face paled, making her green eyes and dark hair stand out in vivid contrast. "I . . . I don't know. We've never done anything like this before."

"I have to do something," Andi said, pinning each of them with a direct look. "When I got home last night, I was handed an eviction notice."

Rachel gasped. "Can you trade your car for cash at one of the local dealers?"

"I can lend you a couple hundred dollars," Kim offered.

"Thanks," Andi said, "but what about rent the following month? And the month after that? A cupcake shop will allow me to do what I love and support my daughter at the same time."

"I'm with you," Rachel agreed, her voice soft but resolute. "You're right. We can do this. And it'll be fun. A fun adventure with my two best friends."

Andi looked at Kim. "Are you in?"

Kim hesitated, then smiled. "Aren't I always?"

THE LOAN OFFICER adjusted his thick, black-framed glasses and motioned toward the plate of cupcakes and three-ring binder Andi placed on the desk in front of him. "What's this?"

"Our business plan."

He flipped open the binder. "It looks like a cookbook."

Andi nodded. "It's meant to be a do-it-yourself cookbook where you add your own recipes to the blank pages. I liked the colorful photos of baked goods on the cover and thought it would be perfect for our new cupcake business. I call it *The Cupcake Diary*, our record of everything cupcake related."

"Isn't it pretty?" Rachel asked.

The loan officer frowned. "A better question is if it's practical."

"After calculating how many cupcakes we'll need to sell each month to cover expenses," Andi said, pointing to one of her many hand drawn graphs, "I put together a budget that includes the rent at the community kitchen on Shipwreck Avenue. I've also researched the cost of equipment for our own shop in the future and ran comparisons between different retailers for supplies."

He barely looked at her or the business plan. His gaze rested on Kim. "And what is your role in this venture?"

Kim's focus was directed toward the other customers

in the bank lobby, and when she didn't respond, Rachel elbowed her.

"What?" Kim asked.

Andi hastily answered for her. "She would help bake and be a cupcake artist."

"What exactly does a 'cupcake artist' do?"

"I can paint using food gels," Kim said, glancing back at him, "create sculptures out of icing, and decorate the cupcakes to be as eye-catching as I can to cultivate more sales."

The loan officer nodded. "Any prior experience working in or running a bakery?"

When Kim shook her head, Andi replied, "No, but I've been baking cupcakes for years. We both have. And Rachel knows every program on the computer and how to advertise online."

The stiff-necked loan officer narrowed his eyes as he took another look at their loan application. "Andrea Leanne Burke. Aren't you that girl who nearly burned down—"

"We can bake," Andi assured him. "All we need is the start-up money to open our business."

Outside, Rachel gave Andi a swift, compassionate look and said, "I'm sorry, Andi. It was worth a try."

"We can't give up," Andi insisted, her tone adamant.

She had to admit she was disappointed when the loan officer listed the reasons for declining a loan. The unpaid bills her deadbeat ex had accrued before the divorce ruined her credit score, Rachel's credit cards were too high, and Kim had no credit at all since she worked under the table through college.

"Did you see the tattoo on the arm of that old guy with the white-haired ponytail, black leather pants, and gray T-shirt?" Kim asked. "It was a flying squirrel. I went up to him in the lobby after you two went out the door, and he says he has a shop on Marine Drive."

"The tattoo guy can't help us get a loan," Rachel complained. "The bank manager was interested in you, and you ignored him. You didn't even try to flirt."

"I'm not going to flirt with the financial manager to get a bank loan. If you like flirting so much, why didn't you flirt with him?"

Rachel sniffed. "He wasn't my type."

"He wasn't Kim's type either," Andi said, putting her arm around her sister's shoulders and giving her a side hug. "You know she hasn't been interested in anyone since Gavin ditched her and ran off to Europe."

"He didn't ditch me." Kim spun around, her eyes wide. "He'd always planned to leave after we graduated college. He asked me to go with him, and I declined. End of story."

"You haven't dated anyone since."

"That's my business."

Rachel pursed her lips. "Speaking of business, how are we going to get the money we need to open a cupcake shop?"

Acquiring financial assistance wasn't as easy as Andi had hoped. They'd have to pursue a more difficult course of action, one that tightened her gut and threatened to squeeze the life right out of her soul. "We'll ask Dad."

Rachel and Kim stared at her for several seconds before Rachel broke the silence. "Is there any hope there?"

"We won't know until we try." Andi stepped off the sidewalk to let a skateboarder pass, and turning her head, she spotted a dented, red Mustang parked in the no parking zone in front of the Zumba Dance Studio. A police officer stood beside the car, an e-citation device in hand. "Rachel, isn't that—"

"No!" Rachel squealed, taking off at a run. "I can't afford a parking ticket!"

"It might help if you flirt with him," Kim teased.

Rachel scowled and waved her hands in an irate fashion that was anything but flirtatious as she tried to persuade the cop to tear the ticket in two.

Andi smiled. "Do you think he's her type?"

"No," Kim said and laughed. "She only likes guys who are interested in her."

"Makes sense. No one wants to waste time with someone who doesn't show a spark of interest."

Andi's thoughts drifted to Jake Hartman, the fine-looking cupcake man. Did Jake have a certain type of woman he was interested in?

Could *she* be his type?

JAKE WAS A thousand times more pleasant to think about than her upcoming meeting with her father. But as much as she detested having to ask her father for a small business loan, she knew it would be better than having to move in with him.

Rachel and Kim agreed to accompany her. But when they arrived at the house, her father quickly singled her out and told them to wait in the other room with Mia.

Andi could smell the negativity in the air the moment she walked in. Her father's opinion of her bounced off the walls and burrowed deep into her heart. She didn't think it was from anything she'd done, but from all the things he thought she should have done and didn't.

He'd expected her to grow up and be a triumphant success. Bring praise to the family name like every Burke listed in the ancestry records before her. Instead, well . . . she hadn't accomplished much.

Andi hoped she was on the cusp of changing that. Profits from a cupcake shop could pay her rent, bring financial independence for herself and her child, and finally allow her to succeed.

She sat down in the small, black leather seat opposite his grandiose, winged-back chair with the gulf of his large formidable, dark mahogany desk positioned between them.

She locked her hands on her knees and prayed for a measure of control over her wavering vocal cords. Then she spilled out her ideas for the cupcake shop, her heart behind each word.

"I suppose you expect me to hand over the money you need for Mia's sake, or the sake of your sister?" he asked.

She'd rehearsed her speech a million times, but none of the words seemed to come out of her mouth the way she'd planned. No, as often occurred on these rare interactions with the man she called Father, her wounded heart regurgitated the past and twisted her tongue.

"Would it be too much to ask you to approve the loan for my sake? I *am* your daughter, too."

"I know exactly who you are, and you don't have the commitment it takes to run a small business."

"If you loan us the money, I'll work days, evenings, weekends, whatever it takes. I've wanted to open some sort of bakery my whole life."

"You don't know what you want. First you want one thing then another. You can't seem to make up your mind. And who would trust you as a baker? You burned cupcakes in your tenth-grade home economics class and set the whole school on fire."

"That was fifteen years ago," Andi said, lifting her chin. "And they weren't cupcakes, they were cinnamon buns."

"To this day everybody in Astoria talks about it."

Andi didn't believe him. *Everybody?* The only person she knew who still talked about the incident was her father. He'd never let her forget how the newspapers had referred to her as 'Pyro-Andi' and 'Burnt Buns Burke.'

"I'm OCD when it comes to kitchen safety now," she said, curling her fingers into a tight squeeze. "I took a food safety test when I applied for the job at the school cafeteria last month, and I passed with flying colors."

"You didn't get the job though, did you? Probably because you never finished college."

"You don't need a degree to work in the school cafeteria," Andi informed him. "And you know why I dropped out of college."

In her third year, her mom had passed away in a small engine plane crash while visiting her aunt and uncle in Idaho. She'd been devastated by the loss. Still was.

"You never went back."

"I decided to do something different."

Her father grimaced. "Yeah, you got married and didn't stay committed to that either."

Andi swallowed hard. "Stuart was the one who didn't stay committed. He cheated on me."

"Every marriage has problems," her father continued. "Your mother and I didn't have a perfect relationship, but we worked it out and remained committed to each other till the day she died. You could have forgiven him and worked to save your marriage."

Andi choked back a sob. "He wouldn't let me! Stuart's the one who filed for the divorce. *He* didn't want to work it out."

She'd never revealed that piece of information to her father before. She'd been too proud. Her eyes stung and her throat ached, burning from the inside. How was it her father was always able to sink his hooks into her and affect her this way?

William Burke shook his head. "You dropped out of college and have had a series of failed jobs, a failed marriage . . ."

Andi waited for him to say it—*failed mom*. Just let him dare say she'd failed as a mom, and she'd leave. Her daughter meant everything to her. She'd do anything to support and protect her.

Only once had she been late to pick Mia up from preschool. She'd been in the bathroom with an upset stomach but to her father it didn't matter. The school had called *him* to come get his granddaughter, and it was yet another incident he'd never let her forget.

"Mom used to say, 'You aren't a failure until you stop trying,'" Andi reminded him.

"Your mother didn't have a wit of sense to save her soul. Did you know she once dreamed of opening a bakery?"

"No, I did not know that," Andi replied in a small voice. "I remember she loved to bake. What happened?"

"I talked some sense into her, that's what happened; convinced her not to make a fool of herself. Baking is one thing, running a business is another. Your mother could never have run a bakery. She had as much business experience as you do."

Andi recalled the happiness on her mother's face when she was in the kitchen, baking cakes and cookies, with flour on her apron. Her heart pined for her mother, to see her one more time. Her mother would have offered encouragement and support and given her the loan. She was sure of it.

"I can do this," Andi said, steeling her resolve. "I will open and run a successful cupcake shop."

"You say you can, but you won't. Right now you've got this big fancy dream—"

"I'll do more than dream." She pushed her chair away from his desk and stood up.

Her father had killed her mother's dream, but she

Chapter Four

Recipe for CUPCAKE SURPRISE

2 scoops of attraction
Several heart-stopping grins
A couple of semi-sweet confessions
A deep layer of "I Must Be Dreaming" intrigue
* Garnish with laughter and unexpected promise.

ON MONDAY RACHEL called, excited, and asked Andi to meet her at the Fish 'N Nets Cafe to discuss a possible new lead for financing the cupcake shop.

Andi couldn't wait to hear the details. After sending Mia off to afternoon kindergarten, she hurried down the paved walk along the waterfront.

Pulling her knit scarf tighter around her neck, to ward off the breezy March chill, she entered the cafe's outside patio. The flavorful aroma of deep-fried fish and chips greeted her nose as she scanned the crowded white round umbrella tables for a wave of Rachel's distinctive flag of red hair.

She found Jake Hartman instead.

He rose from his table, stepped forward, and reached out to shake her hand. "Hi, Andi. Great to see you again."

He knew her name? How did he know her name?

"Rachel should be here soon," Jake continued, "but Kim sent her a text message saying she can't make it."

"You talked to Rachel?"

"Five minutes ago. Would you like to sit?" he asked, motioning a hand toward his table.

"Yes, I think I better," Andi replied. *Before her knees gave out from shock.*

Jake's brown hair and brown eyes appeared lighter this time, glinting with natural golden hues in the outdoor sun. Her gaze slid over his color-coordinated stylish taupe suit, white dress shirt, and loose striped tie, and she sighed. How could a guy so perfectly put together be interested in someone like her?

Yet here he was.

He pulled out a chair for her, and she'd just sat down when Rachel made her appearance, wearing a faded blue designer jacket and matching skirt. If Andi had known she was going to see Jake, she would have worn something similar. Instead she was dressed in jeans and an emerald green Kids Kamp sweatshirt featuring a grizzly bear sleeping in a canoe.

"Here I am," Rachel announced, taking a seat beside her.

"Yes, but what is *he* doing here?" Andi whispered into Rachel's ear.

Rachel grinned. "I invited him."

Andi sucked in her breath. "You didn't! How did you get his number?"

"You left Jake's business card on the table at the restaurant the other night, and I picked it up. You also forgot to take this," Rachel said, handing her the Cupcake Diary with the business plan, "when you stormed out of your father's house yesterday. He gave it to me to give back to you."

Rachel gave Jake a smiling nod and tipped the three-ring binder open at an angle. Andi took a quick peek and discovered Rachel had taped Jake's business card to one of the inside pages. She'd also handwritten a personal note:

You go, girl! Jake's a great catch!

But Rachel still didn't explain why she had called Jake or what he was doing here.

Andi snapped the Cupcake Diary closed, eager for answers.

"I was thinking about the cupcake we ate the other night," Rachel began, "and called Jake to ask about local—"

The LMFAO song "Sexy and I Know It" rang from the cell phone in Rachel's purse, and her eyes lit up. "Excuse me one moment."

Andi slipped a tentative look at Jake while Rachel greeted her caller. He smiled. Was he being friendly, or did his smile consist of something more? She shifted in her seat, her insides tight with excitement, and pretended to study the menu.

"Fantastic!" Rachel exclaimed, then paused, keeping the cell phone against her ear. "Now?" She paused again. "I can be there in fifteen minutes."

Rachel shot up from the table. "I've gotta go."

"Go where?" Andi demanded.

"Down the street," Rachel replied and turned to Jake. "Would you mind if I left you and Andi alone?"

"Not at all," he said with a grin.

Rachel patted Jake's arm as she passed around him. "You *are* sweet."

A lunch date alone with Jake? What would they talk about? Andi swallowed hard. "Rachel, *wait*."

But her friend tossed a you-can-thank-me-later look over her shoulder and left as fast as she'd come.

How could Rachel do this to her? Hadn't she told her a hundred times not to set her up before her heart had time to heal, that she'd start dating again without outside help when she was good and ready?

Jake gave her wrist a light brush with his fingers. "Are you ready?"

Andi stared at him, her skin tingling. "Ready for what?"

"To order."

Jake pointed and when she spun in her seat, she saw the waitress stood behind her.

"Oh. Of course." The aroma wafting toward her from the cafe's kitchen had her salivating for the fried fish and chips. But seeing Jake reminded her she needed to lose a few pounds, and she ordered the tuna salad on whole wheat instead.

"Does the salmon and white bean salad have fresh beans or canned?" Jake asked.

The waitress said, "Canned."

Jake pulled a small notebook out of his shirt pocket and made a note. "Are the tomatoes seeded?"

"No, I'm afraid not."

Jake frowned and made another note. "You know, maybe I should have the halibut sandwich. What kind of dressing does it have?"

"Tartar sauce."

"Plain, no sauce, would be better."

The waitress smiled. "Coming right up."

Jake made a couple more notes in the little black notebook. Seemed like Prince Charming was a picky eater. And what was he writing? Notes about the food? Andi frowned. Would he write notes about her, too?

Her uneasiness grew right after their plates arrived and they began to eat. "The food arrived in exactly fifteen minutes," Jake said, tapping his gold wristwatch. "Good service."

Andi nodded. She'd never timed it, but she'd always thought the cafe was pretty quick. She watched Jake lift the top of his bun with his fork and study the meat. Then he took a bite and made another note in his notebook.

"I'm glad I ordered it plain," Jake said, "so I can get a real grasp of the flavor without the sauce. Tasty, but if I wanted a gourmet sandwich, I might go elsewhere."

Andi stared at him. "Did they ever claim to be gourmet?"

"You're right, they didn't." Again he wrote a note in his

little notebook. "What do you think of the atmosphere?"

"Very judgmental."

He looked up, locked gazes with her, and laughed. "Sorry. When Rachel called to set this up, I suggested we meet here so I could work and talk at the same time."

"Work?"

"I'm a reporter for the *Astoria Sun*," he said, pushing his notebook aside. "Most of my assignments consist of interviews and profile pieces on community events. This week they stuck me in the role of food critic because our regular restaurant reviewer is sick. Except I don't think I'm very good at this. I hate giving bad reviews."

"Like the review for the cupcake we ate the other night at the Captain's Port?" Andi smiled, relieved his critical analysis wasn't an ingrained personality trait.

Jake nodded. "Yes, but it's because of that cupcake that we're here today, isn't it?"

"Maybe that cupcake wasn't so bad after all."

"It was," Jake said, moving his chair closer, "but meeting you made the evening sweeter." He slid her another grin. "So, where would you like to start?"

Andi wasn't as practiced as Rachel at idle chitchat. Better to be up front with the personal facts before either of them wasted any more time . . . or entertained possibilities that would never materialize.

"First," Andi said, taking a deep breath and steeling herself for his reaction, "I think you should know I've got a five-year-old daughter."

"So do I."

"You do?"

"My daughter, Taylor, goes to Astor Elementary."

"So does Mia. I wonder if they know each other."

"Miss Winston's kindergarten?" Jake asked.

Andi nodded. "Have you lived here long? Astoria isn't very big, and I know most of the locals, but I've never seen you around town before."

"We recently relocated from Lake Tahoe. Bought a house near my sister, just a few blocks from here."

"I rent a small Victorian cottage up the hill," Andi told him. "Just me and Mia. My divorce finalized a year ago. And you?"

"Lost my wife to breast cancer when Taylor was three."

"I'm sorry; that must have been hard."

"For you, too."

Andi grimaced. She wasn't sorry she lost her husband. He was still running around with his secretary somewhere in Las Vegas. But it was hard being single again. Lonely.

"I'm glad you came today, Jake."

"You know, I wouldn't be here if I wasn't interested."

Jake gave her a look so soft, so full of emotion, she could barely breathe.

"So? What do you think?" he asked. "Should we take a look at the business plan?"

Andi frowned. "Business plan?"

"For the cupcake shop."

She froze, and the bite of sandwich she'd just put into her mouth turned tasteless. The chatter from the men and women at the surrounding tables drifted away from her ears, and her vision narrowed, excluding all else except the serious expression on Jake's face—the expression of a professional intent on business.

"Andi, are you okay?" Jake placed a hand on her upper arm and gave her a little shake. "Your whole face just went pale. Are you dizzy? Feel faint?"

She shook her head. "I . . . I'll be fine."

"We don't have to go over the details of the partnership today, if you aren't up for it," he said, pulling back.

"Partnership?"

"Rachel gave me most of the numbers over the phone, but we still need to discuss specifics of the business plan before I'd be willing to finance the start-up costs." Jake shot her a hesitant look. "Don't you want me to be your partner?"

Andi covered her eyes with her hand and cringed. "I was under the impression you wanted a different kind of partnership."

Jake was silent for several seconds, then let out a deep, throaty chuckle and pried her hand away from her face. "Did you think Rachel set us up on a date?"

She looked away, unable to face him. How could she have been so foolish? Didn't Rachel say they were meeting here today to discuss a new idea to finance the cupcake shop?

"What if I said one of the reasons I'm interested in financing the cupcake shop is because I *am* interested in you?"

"You barely know me."

"I think I know you better now."

"You don't want to date me. I'm just plain, simple, and

oh-my-gosh, right now I feel so *stupid*."

"How about we start over?" he suggested, taking her hand in his. "Hi, I'm Jake Hartman. I would have asked you out on a date the first night we met, except my babysitter sent a text saying she couldn't watch Taylor past 11:30, and I was already late. I didn't know how you'd react if I asked you out and hit you with the news I'm a father at the same time. Some women hear you have a kid and want to run."

"Some men have been known to do that, too," she said, and shook his hand to formally introduce herself. "Hi, I'm Andi Burke. My dream is to open a cupcake shop with a kitchen big enough to dance in because I love baking. And music. And I also need to pay my rent. But why would such a great financially sound guy like you want to invest his money in a risky venture with a trio of women he doesn't know?"

"Maybe because I, too, have a dream, and with my past experience of owning and operating a restaurant the venture won't be so risky. My family opened a pizzeria when I was growing up, but after my father became ill, we decided to sell the business. Over the last few years I've missed the camaraderie we had as a team. I've been looking to invest in another local restaurant, and when Rachel called asking about Hollande's French Pastry Parlor and told me your plans, I told her I was interested."

"Did she tell you the bank denied our loan?"

Jake nodded. "Banks have to be cautious. Most small businesses fail their first year, but I know what it takes to succeed. Besides," he said and shot her a heart-stopping grin, "I think a gourmet cupcake shop would do well in this town."

"The idea of a fourth business partner hadn't crossed my mind," Andi admitted and smiled, "but I think the idea has merit."

Jake brought her hand up to his mouth and gave it a quick kiss. "I'd also be interested in knowing if you are free on Saturday night to go out on a real date."

"But if we're working together ..." Andi's breath caught in her chest. "Do you think it's wise to mix business with pleasure?"

Jake grinned. "I think we already have."

He was right, of course, but what if mixing the two didn't work out? What then?

As if reading her mind, he added, "If we do this, and you decide our partnership is not working for any reason, you can pay back my investment with future profits, and I will graciously bow out."

Andi hesitated, still unsure.

Her cell phone hummed, shaking the pocket of her baggy sweatshirt. Her first response was to check the ID and make sure it wasn't the school saying Mia had been hurt—her biggest worry. But when she answered, she discovered Rachel had kept another business lead from her.

She looked at Jake. "Rachel says Kim found the perfect place for our shop, and they want us to come see it right away."

"Well then," he said, scooping the Cupcake Diary off the table and offering her his arm, "we better go."

Chapter Five

A dream shared by friends is more fun than dreaming alone.

—Andi

ANDI STOOD BESIDE Rachel and Kim on the sidewalk and surveyed the square brick storefront with two six-by-six-foot street-side windows on either side of the bright red door.

"The door is as red as Rachel's hair," Kim teased.

Rachel pursed her lips. "We can repaint the door."

"I kind of like it," Andi said and pointed to the sign above the shop. "Zeke's Tavern?"

Kim shrugged. "This place was a popular hangout for bikers, but the shopkeeper broke one too many laws and fled."

"I can already see our Creative Cupcakes sign up there," Rachel sang dreamily, her head tilted back, "and the display windows filled with tiers upon tiers of cupcakes in assorted flavors and colors."

"Wait until you see the inside," Kim said, her face aglow. "There's already a kitchen and a big marble customer counter, tables, and chairs. The previous tenant left a lot of equipment behind that the building owner said we could use."

"Sorry I didn't tell you about this when Kim called me away from lunch," Rachel whispered against Andi's ear. "I thought you'd like the chance to stay and get to know Jake. Am I right?"

Jake had driven her to the shop in his shiny blue convertible Mazda Miata and stood inside the doorway, talking with the owner of the building about the lease.

"I forgive you," Andi told Rachel with a smile, "but no more secrets." Next she turned toward her sister. "Kim, how did you find this place?"

"The tattoo guy I met at the bank said he had a shop on Marine Drive. I tried to find it to see more of his designs but found this place instead. The owner of the building was cleaning out the inside for a new tenant, and I asked him about renting the space to us. Come take a look."

Kim led the way, swinging her slender arms with a flourish while pointing to all the interior walls. "My paintings can decorate the shop and be available for purchase at the same time. It really will be like having my own art gallery."

Andi had never seen her quiet, aloof sister so animated.

She had to admit the excitement was contagious. Her heart skipped a beat the moment she stepped into the spacious adjoining kitchen and opened all the cupboards and drawers. Her resolve to make Creative Cupcakes a success grew stronger with every passing moment, and her hope for the future soared.

Once the beer advertisements were taken down and the shop was cleaned up and painted, it would be perfect. They could redecorate with sheer pink curtains, install glass display cases, and line the whole back countertop with cupcake boxes.

A wide door toward the back of the room piqued her interest, and she flung it open. "What's this?"

Her loud audible gasp brought Rachel, Kim, Jake, and the building owner to her side.

Kim's mouth popped open. "It's the tattoo parlor!"

Andi stared at the tattoo patterns pasted to the walls, the dentist-style chairs, and the tattoo guns, needles, and colorful tubes of ink next to the jar of Vaseline on the back table.

"He's on vacation this week," the building owner told them.

"His door connects to this shop?" Jake asked with a look of concern.

The building owner nodded, and Andi glanced at the others' faces. Each of them displayed different shades of unspoken doubt.

"No wonder I couldn't find the shop earlier," Kim said, her eyes growing wide. "I didn't think to look behind the building."

"Cupcakes and tattoos do not mix!" Andi exclaimed, imagining her father's reaction if he found out.

Rachel patted her arm and stuck her head farther into the dim back room. "It isn't as bad as you think. The tattoo shop has its own side door."

"His customers can also come through our section in the front," Andi said apprehensively, "and scare everyone away."

"A tattoo shop wouldn't scare me away," Rachel argued. "What do you have against tattoos?"

"Tattoo parlors are not kid friendly and family oriented. Do you think I want Mia hanging out with a bunch of black-leather, bald-headed bikers with inked-up skin?"

"Not everyone with a tattoo wears black leather," Rachel teased. "I bet in a month's time little Mia and the tattoo artist will become great friends."

"He's an artist, I'm an artist, and baking is an art form, too," Kim added. "As fellow artists, I think we should stick together and find a way to work this out."

"Jake?" Andi asked. "What do you think?"

"Every business venture includes a certain amount of risk," he said, looking her in the eye. "But the front of the building *is* the ideal space for a cupcake shop, and you can't beat the location."

Andi looked out the large front windows to the tall steel girder trusses of Astoria's biggest attraction, the Astoria–Megler Bridge, the longest continuous truss bridge in North America. Below, the glistening water of the Columbia River beckoned and would offer an amazing view to their customers, especially if they were tourists.

She glanced at Rachel and Kim, and they both nodded.

"Okay," Andi said, replacing her reservations with a rueful grin. "Let's talk business."

SEVERAL HOURS LATER, after going over the fine details with Jake and the building owner, Andi added her signature below everyone else's on the lease agreement. She couldn't be certain which excited her more: opening her own cupcake shop or the fact she'd see their new partner, Jake, on a daily basis.

While Rachel and Kim checked out more of the kitchen, Andi swooped around the large front marble counter. "Can I take your order, please?"

Jake took a stool on the opposite side reserved for customers. "I'll take a hot fudge sundae cupcake with spicy dark chocolate frosting and chocolate sprinkles. My new girlfriend loves chocolate."

"Girlfriend?" Andi arched an eyebrow. "I didn't know you had a girlfriend."

"Well, she hasn't given me her phone number yet," Jake said, a glint in his eye, "but I'm hoping she will, once she figures out if we should date or not."

Andi smiled and averted her gaze. "My phone number is on your copy of the business papers we signed."

"I know, but it's not the same. If *you* give it to me, I'll know it's okay to call to ask you out."

"You can call," she said, her voice wavering, "but . . . let's see how we all work together first."

Jake studied her a moment, and a solemn expression

crossed over his face. "Does the word 'date' scare you, Andi?"

"It does." Heat rose into her cheeks, and she gave a little high-pitched laugh. "I haven't '*dated*' since my divorce."

Jake circled around the marble counter to stand by her side. "How about we meet here Saturday night, say it's a business meeting, and order pizza?"

Andi looked up into his warm eyes, and her heart leaped in her chest. "Okay."

"Okay?" Jake said and grinned.

"Yes. Oh, Jake, can you believe it? Our very own cupcake shop!" Andi spread her arms wide and twirled around.

Jake caught her hand in his and gave her a couple of extra twirls. "With a kitchen big enough to dance in."

"Thank you for helping us," Andi said, coming to a stop in his arms and resting her hands on his chest. "I won't let you down. I plan to make this shop a huge success."

"Don't you mean 'we'?"

"Of course. *We* will make the shop a success." With her spirits soaring higher than they had in days, Andi tore a slip of paper from the Cupcake Diary, wrote down her phone number, and pressed it into his hand. "See you Saturday, Jake."

ANDI, RACHEL, AND Kim worked long hours over the next seven days to clean, paint, decorate, and prepare

Creative Cupcakes for customers. Lucky for them the shop had come with much of the furnishings, and Andi had already spent years perfecting baking methods and testing recipes. Jake purchased an industrial mixer and glass display case from a restaurant supplier, Rachel discovered the perfect website from which to order pink personalized cupcake boxes, and Kim practiced her artistic skills with frosting.

Mia helped in the mornings, as much as a five-year-old could, then Andi would put her on the bus for afternoon kindergarten and work some more before the bus dropped her daughter back off again. Heather took Mia home early and helped put her to bed. But Andi stayed into the evening, when Jake would arrive and do what he could to lend a hand.

This week Mia had off from school for spring break and sat quietly at one of the shop's round white dining tables coloring with crayons in one of her Disney cartoon books.

"This was Mom's recipe," Andi said, showing Rachel and Kim how to mix the ingredients for lemon-coconut cupcakes. "Do you think our shop menu should start with twelve different flavors?"

Kim added the last cup of sugar to the bowl. "No more than that or we'll get overwhelmed."

"How early do you think we'll have to get up in the morning to start baking every day?" Rachel asked, leaning against the counter full of flour, sugar, eggs, butter, brown sugar, coconut, and vanilla.

Andi laughed. "Earlier than *you're* used to."

She turned on the electric mixer, and the buzz of the swirling beaters deafened their ears for several long minutes. Then Andi shut off the machine and filled the individual cups of the baking tray with the yellow batter. She'd insisted on buying the thicker cupcake wrappers, even though they cost more, to keep the edges of the cupcakes straight and sturdy. Seemed like a good choice.

"What I want to know," Rachel said, her full red lips curving up into a devious smile, "is if it was a business meeting, then why weren't Kim and I invited?"

Andi flushed, thinking of her night at the cupcake shop with Jake. They'd talked and talked, ordered pizza, baked a batch of cupcakes, and talked a whole lot more. She evaded her friend's question and instead replied, "Jake found a supplier who sells second-hand baking equipment for half price. Isn't that nice?"

"The tattoo artist is nice," Kim said, gathering some of the used bowls, measuring cups, and spoons and depositing them into the sink. "His name is Guy."

Rachel laughed. "A nice Guy?"

The back door connecting the cupcake shop with the tattoo parlor burst open, and a large dark-haired man, wearing a ripped denim vest and a wild look in his eye, ran into the room. Two uniformed cops chased behind him, the larger one knocking the man to the floor face down, and locking metal cuffs on him behind his back.

Mia screamed, and Andi flew to her daughter and swept her up in her arms.

"You didn't even let Guy finish," the arrested man

complained, as the two police officers pulled him from the floor to his feet.

The officer who'd knocked him down said, "Tough."

Rachel gasped. "You're the same cop who wrote me the parking ticket!"

The big square-jawed cop with short sandy hair who reminded Andi of a Rock 'em Sock 'em Robot glanced toward her friend and nodded. "Good to see you."

Rachel frowned. "Wish I could say the same."

After the two officers escorted the man from the building, Andi released her daughter and opened the Cupcake Diary on the counter of their new cupcake shop. Clenching her teeth, her shaky fingers picked up a pen and wrote:

Never rush into a commitment.

"Andi, don't say it," Kim warned, holding up her hand. "I admit maybe we should have taken more time to think about the decision to open our shop next to the tattoo parlor."

"Too late now," Rachel said, wincing. "We already signed the lease."

Andi groaned. "This is a disaster!"

"There's more bad news." Rachel held up her cell phone to show them her latest phone message. "The health inspector can't come and approve the kitchen until the end of the month."

Andi's thoughts shot to her Victorian cottage on the hill. "That means we won't be open in time to make a profit to help me pay my rent."

"I can help."

Andi turned around to find the white-ponytailed tattoo artist, inked with designs from the neck down, standing behind her, and she jumped with a start. "I didn't see you."

He grinned and revealed a gaping hole where his left canine tooth was missing. "Sorry. They say I move quiet as a ghost through walls."

"That's supposed to make me feel better?" she asked.

"No, maybe not. But if I get the health department to move up your inspection date, would you accept that as an apology for my customer and his uniformed friends' intrusion?"

Andi didn't know what to say, but Rachel and Kim agreed, and Guy went off to make the call.

"Maybe one of the health inspectors is a client of his," Kim whispered. "Maybe he's calling in a favor."

"Someone he knows well enough to bribe?" Rachel added. "Someone with a dirty little secret to hide?"

Andi exchanged a dire look with her now wide-eyed friend and then her pale-faced sister. "Maybe we don't want to know."

Guy walked back toward them and handed the phone to Andi. "It's all set for noon tomorrow. She wants to talk to you to confirm."

"Who?"

"My cousin," he said, waving to Mia, who peeked at him timidly from around the end of the counter. "She's one of the local health inspectors and a struggling mom trying to make ends meet. Just like you. She agreed to come on her lunch hour if we provide the lunch."

Andi tried not to let her mouth fall open. "She—your cousin—she did?"

"Thank you, Guy," Kim said, shaking his hand. "We are all so glad we're going to be your next-door neighbors, aren't we, girls?"

Rachel nodded, and Andi had to agree. "Glad to have you with us, Guy."

Chapter Six

Recipe for Success: let your dream rise above your fear of failure.

—Jake Hartman, cupcake critic

ANDI'S MOVEMENTS CONTAINED a little sway as she push-pinned the Creative Cupcakes business license to the front wall of the shop. True to his word, Guy's cousin had moved up their health department inspection and given the shop county approval to open for business.

Next, Andi turned to the page in the Cupcake Diary where she'd pasted a recipe for strawberry milkshake cupcakes and found a handwritten note from Rachel.

I changed the oven temperature to 350° on the last batch. See if you notice a difference.

P.S. Jake wanted to know your favorite color, and I said yellow. Was I right? I bet you get a bouquet of yellow roses. Or tulips. Tulips are in season for Easter. So are daffodils. What a guy! Can you ask him if he has any good-looking single friends?

Andi smiled, picked up a pen, and wrote: *Will do.* Then she placed the diary back under the counter for Rachel to read later.

She glanced about the room to see if everything was in place for their first day. Mia had been picked up earlier to play at a friend's house. Kim was using her artistry to create flower petals out of a batch of purple and pink frosting. Rachel was on her laptop at one of the round white tables sending announcements to every social media site, loop, and group that Creative Cupcakes was now open for business. Or would be—in about five more minutes. And Jake was assisting his tech friend, Caleb, whom he'd recruited from a local media crew, to install their new security camera.

After the arrest of Guy's customer the week before, Andi wasn't taking any chances on Mia's safety. She'd insisted acquisition of a camera become number one on their to-do list. Caleb stood on a ladder and set the security camera on the plant shelf in the far corner so it could film the interior of the shop and face the front door.

"Ready for our first customer?" Jake asked, turning the OPEN sign around on the front window to face the street.

"Ready!" Andi, Rachel, and Kim answered in unison.

Ten minutes later a short, middle-aged man walked in and bought four of their Key lime cupcakes frosted with fresh whipped cream and topped with graham cracker crumbs and lime rind strips.

Rachel gave him a big smile and almost bounced up and down while placing his order into the pink cardboard cupcake box. Kim handed him extra napkins and a coupon to come back. Andi took his money and placed it in the cash register, which opened with a high-pitched *ker-ching*. The sweet sound of success.

Jake drew near as the man went back out the door. "Very good, ladies, but next time you might not want to hover. I think you made him nervous."

Rachel went back to her laptop and asked, "Andi, can you come take a look at the new website before I upload?"

Andi started to make her way over when a sudden rise in voices erupted from outside.

She glanced past their new OPEN sign on the window to the crowd of women forming on the sidewalk. One of the women carried a metal garbage can. Another held the can's lid and struck it with a long wooden spoon.

The clamor brought everyone inside the cupcake shop to the front window, including Guy, who came in from the tattoo parlor.

Rachel frowned. "What's with all the signs?"

"Protesters," Kim warned, "and they don't look friendly."

"What could they be protesting?" Andi read one of the signs and gasped. "Cupcakes?"

Guy let out a chuckle. "They never protested tattoos

or Zeke's old bar, but cupcakes? Looks like they're against devil's food."

The protesters consisted of four women, all wearing the same colorful outfits: black tank tops and teal rip-stop nylon pants, complete with bright red, yellow, and blue mesh tassels attached to each side and hanging off each back pocket.

"What the heck are the tassels for?" Andi muttered.

Rachel smirked. "To twirl around when they shake their booty."

The woman with short black hair seemed to be in charge, the other three her groupies. She wore a short top and low-cut pants, leaving her tight midriff exposed. Andi had to admit the woman was a poster child for fitness even though her facial lines were those of a forty-year-old. She blocked the short little man who had been in the cupcake shop minutes before and pointed to the garbage can.

"Drop the cupcakes and drop the sugar in your diet," the lead woman commanded, her raised voice distinct through the large glass window.

"Don't you want to be healthy?" asked another woman closing in on him.

The man's forehead creased and his eyes widened. "I paid sixteen dollars for these cupcakes."

"You'll pay with your life if you eat all that sugar," the black-haired woman assured him. "Did you know sugar is addicting?"

"No, I didn't." The man took a quick glance to the left and then to the right as the women surrounded him, waving their picket signs.

A brunette wearing a neon green mesh kerchief over the top of her hair pointed again. "Drop it in the can, buddy. Do the right thing."

Clearly intimidated, the poor man dropped the box of cupcakes in the can and hurried away. The women clapped, cheered, and broke into a hip-hop dance across the sidewalk.

Next, the four women prevented a young couple from entering the shop, shoved an orange slip of paper into their hands, and chanted, "Cupcakes can kill! Cupcakes can kill!"

"They're terrorizing, blocking, and forcing flyers into our customer's hands," Kim whispered, her expression turning fierce. "All of which is illegal."

"That's it," Andi growled under her breath as she flung open the door and went with Rachel and Kim on her heels.

Rachel gasped. "Who *are* these people?"

"Zumba dancers," Kim said, pointing to another sign. "They're from the studio around the block. 'Lose the fat, dance with Pat.'"

Andi took a deep breath. She had been thinking of signing up for that Zumba dance class, but no way would she take it now. She scanned each of their colorful outfits. "Which one of you is Pat?"

The lead woman with short black hair and exposed midriff waved. "I'm Pat Silverthorn," she said, fingering a silver whistle that dangled from a cord around her neck.

Andi nodded to her. "You need to stop this nonsense right now."

Pat gave her a sly grin and shouted, "Give up the sugar!" and blew the whistle twice. The dancers circled with their signs, and at the signal, they changed their rhythm to a salsa.

"Maybe we should have opened a health food store," Kim said and shied away when one of the women drew near.

Andi shook her head. "This is ridiculous."

"Oh, no," Jake said, his grim tone full of foreboding as he came through the door to stand behind them. "That's my sister."

"Pat?"

"No, the one with the brown hair and green head scarf."

The woman he indicated dropped her sign. "Jake, what are you doing here?"

"I financed this shop, and you and your entourage are scaring away business."

"I had no idea you were part of this. Couldn't you have picked a shop with real food to invest in?"

Jake motioned Andi over and said, "Andi, this is my sister, Trish."

The woman's expression froze. "Oh, I see how it is. You *like* her."

Jake nodded. "I do. Andi is a very nice person."

"She's more than that, isn't she, Jake? You can't fool me. I haven't seen that look in your eyes since Taylor was born. You're infatuated with her."

Infatuated? Andi spun around so fast her head nearly collided with Jake's. His jaw twitched, but she didn't know him well enough to see if his sister spoke the truth. And instead of confirming the comment, he chose to ignore it.

"Can you stop picketing and leave our customers alone?" he asked, as his sister's Zumba friends surrounded another potential customer.

"Can you stop selling sugar and show our diabetic father some support?"

As Jake continued to argue with his sister, Kim asked, "What do we do now?"

"Call the cops," Rachel said, taking out her cell phone.

Andi agreed, and minutes later, a patrol car pulled up to the curb, and the same two police officers who had come to their shop before got out.

Kim smiled. "Look, Rachel, it's your friend."

Rachel rolled her eyes. "Don't they have any other cops on the force?"

The large, square-jawed cop with the short blond hair introduced himself as Officer Ian Lockwell, and the two officers began to question Pat, who did not appear pleased.

"I have no problem booking you all," Officer Lockwell said. "If you want to have your protest, fine. But, you cannot interfere with foot traffic nor can you interfere with the operation of this business with your disorderly conduct."

"Our conduct is *not* disorderly," Pat argued. "We dance in distinct patterns."

"You're blocking the entrance and exit of a store."

"We're educating the public." Pat poked a finger into

his large stomach. "Looks like you could use a little education about good nutrition, too."

"You poke that finger at me again, and the next time you use it will be to push the number of your one call for bail."

"On what charge?" Pat demanded.

Officer Lockwell leaned in. "Battery on a police officer."

"My mother died with a box of triple chocolate gourmet cupcakes sitting in her lap," Pat informed him. "People have a right to know an unhealthy diet can be lethal."

"Then educate the public someplace else."

"We will," Pat said, her face smug. "My Zumba class is leading the opening exercises at the Relay for Life fundraiser this weekend."

With a signal from Pat, the Zumba dancers dropped their picket signs and stepped aside to let Creative Cupcakes customers pass by.

Andi was relieved, but the smiles that she, Rachel, and Kim exchanged with Officer Lockwell quickly faded. They'd gained a new friend, but they'd also gained a new enemy.

"I'm not going to give up," Pat hissed over her shoulder as she walked away, "not until Creative Cupcakes closes for business."

"I think she means it," Rachel said, her voice raw.

"Doesn't she have anything better to do?" Kim complained.

"No, but we do." Andi picked up an orange half-page

flyer one of the women had dropped on the ground. "The Relay for Life fundraiser for cancer research draws hundreds of people each year."

Rachel's mouth popped open. "The perfect venue for a new cupcake shop to advertise."

"And help the community at the same time," Kim added.

"Who says cupcakes can't be healthy?" Andi asked, handing them the flyer. "We can bake low-calorie, low-sugar, gluten-free, and even fruit and vegetable cupcakes. We can promote health awareness. But even more important," she said, balling her fists, "we're going to prove Creative Cupcakes has a place in this town."

Chapter Seven

Relay for Life Fundraiser Checklist

800 mini cupcakes, each color frosting representing
    a different type of cancer
Plastic stackable trays to transport cupcakes in back
    of car
Calculator and pouch with small change
Napkins (lots of napkins!)

ON FRIDAY NIGHT Andi, Rachel, and Kim closed Creative Cupcakes at five o'clock and set up their tented booth at the Relay for Life fundraiser. The event, usually held in June, had been moved up to mid-March to accommodate needed repairs to both the high school track and the encircling football field.

"We look like Easter eggs," Kim complained, tying on her purple apron. "Whose idea was it to wear purple?"

"Mine," Rachel informed her. "Purple represents pancreatic cancer. In memory of my grandmother."

"The scarves can also help keep us warm," Andi

said, taking the purple scarf Rachel handed her. "The spring chill will make people walk even faster this evening."

Andi had no history of cancer in her family and had never fully understood why people walked to raise money for cancer research. But as she watched a young mother pushing her daughter around in a wheelchair, a cancer victim no older than Mia, she realized it was because they could. What an amazing gift it was to have the ability to walk. To live life. And to help others.

The stories she overheard of hardship and survival made her want to hug her child more, laugh with Rachel and Kim more, spend more time with Jake . . .

She missed Jake. Despite her reluctance to allow herself to commit to a serious relationship, she couldn't stop thinking about him. He worked at the newspaper during the day and helped out at the cupcake shop every night, but she hadn't spent time alone with him since the previous weekend. And five days seemed like an eternity. She kept her eye on the crowd, hoping to see him.

Instead, Pat, accompanied by twenty other women, all wearing pink tassels for breast cancer, visited their multi-colored cupcake display.

Pat gave a smile too fake to be real. "We just wanted to stop by and wish you luck."

"Wish us luck?" Rachel grumbled as the Zumba dancers moved on. "What's with her abrupt attitude change?"

"She must be up to something," Kim warned. "I don't trust her."

"I don't either," Andi admitted, "but what can she possibly do to us here?"

A line of customers formed in front of their booth and Rachel turned toward her with a frown. "This guy has a coupon for a free cupcake. What do I do?"

Andi looked at the slip of paper Rachel handed her. "The people in charge of the fundraiser may have issued a few coupons to the public. Go ahead and give him one."

However, a short time later they were inundated with dozens of these coupons.

"Why wasn't I told about this?" Andi demanded.

Kim served four more free cupcakes to the kids lined up in front of them. "You made sure we get to keep the money we spent on supplies, right?"

"That's what I was told," Andi assured her.

"We won't recoup any money for supplies if this keeps up," Rachel complained. "And we aren't raising any money for cancer research."

"Look there!" Kim pointed. "The Zumba dancers are the ones handing out the coupons to everyone. They're trying to sabotage our efforts!"

"Not if I can help it," Andi said, pulling off her disposable food handler's gloves.

Marching up to the stadium stands where a jazz band had just performed, she took the microphone. "I'm sorry to announce that due to a misprint, the Creative Cupcakes coupons are invalid. The purpose of the fundraiser is to *raise* money. Please stop by and buy a sampling of our many different flavors, only a dollar each for a mini cupcake."

DESPITE THE INITIAL loss, Andi, Rachel, and Kim quickly recouped the money with continuing sales. And although they made sure to include health-conscious varieties like carrot and gluten-free espresso, the fastest selling were the chocolate caramel, cream-filled s'mores, and Easter candy cupcakes topped with jelly beans.

"Andi, look at that woman's victory sword." Kim nodded to the celebration for cancer survivors taking place at the center of the field. "It looks like a shiny gold cake cutter."

"I'll have to ask her where to get one," Rachel said with a grin, "so we can celebrate our own victory."

Andi smiled, but her stomach remained tight. It was a little early to claim any kind of victory. Two weeks remained in the month, and their profits hadn't been enough to even cover expenses. And she still needed to pay her back rent.

"The day we don't have to work sixteen-hour shifts will be success enough," Andi said, her tone weary.

"My only complaint," Rachel teased, "is that most of the single men at this event are in high school. Not a great place to pick up a hot date."

"Sorry, Rach—" Andi looked up, straight into Jake's eyes, and it was almost as if he could look right through her and see her exhaustion. The compassion on his face made her heart flutter.

"Can you take a break to walk around the track with me?" Jake asked.

"Of course she can," Rachel said, giving her a little push. "We can handle this crowd. Right, Kim?"

"It seems to be winding down," Kim agreed. "Everyone's getting ready to light up the luminary bags to honor the cancer victims."

"Thanks, you two," Andi said and whisked off her apron.

Jake wore jeans and an emerald green sweatshirt over a white T-shirt, and to Andi, he'd never looked better. The clothes could not hide the fact he had a great athletic build, with toned muscles in all the right places.

"I knew you must exercise to look so good." She caught herself and corrected, "I mean—look so fit."

Jake's lips twitched as if he were suppressing a grin. "I don't walk as much as I'd like to," he said and shot her an earnest look of appeal. "Maybe if I had someone to walk with, I'd find the time. Would you like to walk with me on Sunday?"

She cocked her head to one side. "Are you asking for a date?"

"Since you're opposed to dates, why don't we call it 'spending time with each other to share our appreciation for similar interests'?"

"I'm interested," Andi said.

Jake smiled. "So am I."

Together Andi and Jake joined the hundreds of other people circling the track. Some belonged to teams who handed off decorated batons to each other. Some danced to the pumped up rock music. And others were drawn toward the strong, delicious smell of hot dogs and popcorn, which tested Andi's willpower on her new diet.

Halfway around the track they met Heather with Mia, both behind a table braiding friendship bracelets.

"Look, Mom," Mia said, running up to her with their donation jar. "We sold lots!"

"Great." Andi swooped down and wrapped Mia in a hug. "But in twenty minutes, I want you to come back to the cupcake booth. It's almost time to go home."

"Heather said people walk all night."

"They do," Andi replied, tousling her daughter's hair. "But not us. We need to go to bed."

"Who's he?" Mia asked, her eyes on Jake.

"This is the man who helped us open the cupcake shop. His name is Jake Hartman."

Jake knelt down to Mia's level and offered her a handshake. "Nice to meet you, Mia. My daughter, Taylor, is in your class at school."

"Taylor?" Mia sucked in her breath, her blue eyes filling with tears, and turned to Andi. "She stole the Gummy Bears you gave me and called me stupid."

"I'm sure she didn't mean it," Andi said, sneaking a peak at Jake's shocked expression.

"She did," Mia shot back, her lower lip quivering. "I hate her."

"Now, Mia," Andi warned, her voice firm, "you know we don't *hate* anybody. Don't you have anything to say to Jake?"

Mia gave Jake a wary glance.

"Something nice?" Andi prompted.

"You can't be as bad as she is," Mia said, shaking his hand. Then she ran back to the table with Heather.

Jake cleared his throat. "Well, that's good to know."

Andi cringed. "I'm sorry. Mia's tired and shouldn't be up this late."

"Don't worry; you get to meet my daughter next, and you've already been warned about her temperament."

Jake smiled, but from his expression it was clear he meant to talk to his daughter about her actions. Andi meant to speak to Mia also and hoped they might find a way to all be friends.

Three-quarters of the way around the track Jake stopped in front of his sister, Trish, and introduced her husband, Oliver, and their son, Evan. Then he introduced his own daughter, Taylor.

Jake's sister, still wearing her pink ribbons and pink-tasseled Zumba pants, gave Andi a hard look. "Oh, no."

Jake squinted at her with concern. "What's wrong?"

"She's looking at you the same way I saw you looking at her the other day," Trish said, rolling her eyes.

Jake gave a quick half-turn, but Andi hid her face by stepping forward to greet his daughter. Taylor had Jake's and his sister's brown hair, but her eyes were lighter, filling with tears the same way Mia's had.

"Did you know my mom?" Taylor asked.

"No, I didn't," Andi admitted.

"We made a bag for her," Taylor explained.

Andi glanced at the white paper bag lantern on the ground by their feet, decorated with crayon-colored hearts stickers, and illuminated by the tea candle inside.

The name SUSAN HARTMAN was written on the front, with a photo of a beautiful woman with dark wavy hair below it.

Jake had said his wife had passed away two years ago when Taylor was three, but Andi got the feeling she shouldn't be here. At this event. With them.

No wonder Jake hadn't taken her hand as they walked. He was here to honor his deceased wife. To hold hands with another would be inappropriate. Awkward. Still . . . as they stood side by side, her hand itched to take his and close the four-inch gap keeping them apart. And for that, a strong dose of guilt set in, making her even more uncomfortable.

The lights in the stadium went off, leaving them in the dark except for the warm, golden glow from the vast ring of luminaries around the track. There were hundreds of them. Each one decorated and lit as a memorial to a loved one who had battled cancer. Andi caught her breath. The moment was surreal, both beautiful and sad, yet it also ignited a steadfast hope for the future. A future with a cure. A future spent with loved ones. Jake's warm fingers found her hand and gave it a quick squeeze.

"I'm glad you're here with me," he murmured in her ear.

The queasiness in Andi's stomach subsided, and she relaxed.

"I'm glad, too," she whispered.

WHEN ANDI CAME back to the cupcake booth, her heart was as light as a feather. "What a great walk! I think I've lost ten pounds already."

"Lost your heart," Kim teased.

"Lost her resolve not to get involved," Rachel added.

"Lost track of time," Andi said, glancing at her watch. "I didn't mean to be gone so long."

"We can't complain," Rachel told her. "We know you were just trying to make our Creative Cupcakes' investor happy."

Kim gave her a mischievous smile. "Is he happy?"

"Yes," Andi affirmed, "I believe he is."

The music coming over the PA system stopped, and a female voice echoed across the stadium thanking sponsors and various vendors for their support.

"We'd especially like to thank Creative Cupcakes for raising over one thousand dollars for cancer research."

The roar of clapping echoed around the stadium and drowned out Andi's horrified gasp.

Rachel glared at her. "I thought you said we could deduct our expenses from the sales."

"That's what the woman on the phone told me," Andi whispered.

"What woman?" Kim asked. "The announcer woman? Look at her outfit. She's one of Pat's Zumba dancers!"

Andi hesitated. "I can tell her there's been a mistake."

"There's no mistake," Rachel said, scrunching her face. "Pat's Zumba tribe planned this all along, and we just lost several hundred dollars on ingredients."

Andi ran up into the stadium stands and took the microphone for the second time that night. "Creative Cupcakes was *thrilled* to be part of this event," she said, shooting a look at the pink-tasseled announcer. "And we hope everyone will keep us in mind for future weddings, family reunions, and school birthday parties."

Pat walked past Andi and smirked. "Fat chance."

Chapter Eight

I could give up chocolate, but I'm not a quitter.

—**Author unknown**

By Wednesday Andi was shocked that after all the cupcakes they gave away over the weekend, the customers
coming into the shop were few. In fact, some people who
had placed orders the previous week for school birthday parties called and canceled. She tapped the calendar
hanging on the wall beside the phone with her pencil.
Eleven days remained in the month. Eleven days . . .

One of Guy's customers came through the connecting
back door and bought one of her sister's painted confec-
tions.

Kim had discovered how to cover the cupcakes with
white fondant, which created a smooth porcelain-like

base. Then using various sized brushes, she painted scenes on the surface using different colored edible pastes mixed with clear flavored extract. Some of the paintings were replicas of her own artwork, and some, like the one this man ordered, she'd copied from one of Guy's tattoo designs.

He nodded his thanks in appreciation of the hand-painted Harley-Davidson. Then he lifted the side edge of the white bandage on his upper arm and nodded to Kim. "You like?"

Andi and Kim, both behind the counter, exchanged a look and laughed. His freshly applied tattoo was a pink-frosted cupcake.

The front door opened, and Officer Lockwell entered, sat down at the counter, and ordered their newest flavor—a delicacy of vanilla topped with maple syrup and bacon. The man with the new tattoo made a quick exit.

"Looks like you scared him away," Andi said, placing the police officer's order in front of him. "The tattoo parlor hasn't seen as many customers since you started coming in every day."

"Is the tattoo artist complaining?" Officer Lockwell asked.

"A little," Andi admitted.

"Tell him I can't help it," Officer Lockwell confided with a grin. "Every night when I get home my wife and kids ask if I've brought them more cupcakes. They love them."

Rachel came in from the kitchen, gave Officer Lockwell a hesitant wave, then slapped a bridal magazine on the counter in front of them. "You have to see this. I found a company that sells long-handled, gold-plated cake knives."

Andi glanced at their potential "victory" cupcake cutter, but her gaze couldn't help straying to the opposite page, which featured an array of dazzling diamond wedding rings.

No way was she ready to remarry, but the sight of the rings brought warm, fuzzy feelings to life inside her and made her think of Jake. Her fanciful daydreams carried her through the day, but they came to an end the moment Mia got off the school bus, her eyes streaming with tears.

Andi dropped to her knees on the sidewalk outside the cupcake shop and took her daughter into her arms. "Mia, what happened?"

"They said I can't bring cupcakes to school for my birthday!"

"Who said?" Andi asked, pulling Mia away to look at her again. "Your teacher?"

Mia nodded, and more tears spilled from her eyes. "Hannah and John had cupcakes, but the teacher told me I can't have any cupcakes."

"That can't be right. I'm sure there's a mistake. I'll call the school and straighten everything out."

Andi escorted Mia into the shop and reached for the phone. A minute later she was on the line with Mia's teacher, and five minutes after that she was transferred to the principal, who explained the situation.

"Last night Pat Silverthorn convinced the school board to ban cupcakes from all the district schools. She presented a long list of facts, backed by clinical studies finding that sugar is the number one cause of obesity in children. By allowing the children to bring cupcakes to school on their birthday or any other celebration, we would be supporting the current obesity epidemic. The school board has decided we can't be responsible for putting children's health at risk."

"We're talking about a child's birthday!" Andi said indignantly. "If you're going to start a rule like that, can't you wait until the beginning of the next school year? My daughter feels that everyone else has been able to celebrate their birthday in school except her."

"A child does not need cupcakes to celebrate a birthday, Ms. Burke."

"Try explaining that to a five-year-old," Andi retorted.

After she hung up, she turned to her daughter, who stood staring into the display case. "Mia, I'm sorry they won't let you bring cupcakes to school to share with your class, but we can celebrate your birthday right here in the shop. We can decorate, and you can invite all your friends."

"What if they don't come?"

Andi had once suffered the humiliation of sitting alone in a coffee shop waiting for a blind date to show, and it hadn't even been her birthday. She'd always had Rachel and Kim to celebrate with for as long as she could remember. But Mia had no siblings and hadn't yet met many friends.

"They'll come," Andi promised her, "because we'll make your birthday too much fun to miss. And I know one classmate who will definitely come."

Mia wiped her eyes. "Who?"

"Jake's daughter, Taylor."

Mia cringed. "I don't like Taylor."

"Why not?"

"She's mean."

"How is she *mean*?"

"She sits with Priscilla and sticks her tongue out at me."

"Priscilla?"

"Priscilla Silverthorn."

Andi groaned. No doubt Priscilla was the Zumba instructor's daughter. And if Pat convinced the school board to ban cupcakes, then that must be the reason so many people had called to cancel their orders for upcoming birthdays. She had to admit, Pat was resourceful. And obstinate. She just kept pushing, pushing, pushing and refused to give up.

If Andi didn't push back and do something to stop her, Pat would push them right out of business. And once again, Andi would have to listen to her father call her a failure, or at least imply it. What she needed was a plan, another way to bring customers into the shop.

She watched Mia wander behind the cupcake counter and put a white baker's hat on her head. That was it! What if she created an after-school kid's program, a cupcake camp for kids? They could push some of the tables in the back of the shop together to create the proper workspace and she could hire Heather to man the cash register so she, Rachel, and Kim could teach the children to make cupcakes.

The next day, Andi sent Mia to school with invitations for her entire kindergarten class to come join in the new after-school program, Future Bakers of Astoria. For a ten-dollar fee, they could come for two hours, learn to bake, and decorate four mini cupcakes to take home.

That afternoon only three kids came. The following day there were eight. On Saturday fifteen arrived, their parents delighted to have two hours free to run errands and take advantage of some much needed alone time.

Andi recognized a couple of the mother's from Pat's Zumba dance class. Officer Lockwell brought his son and daughter to the event. And even Jake's sister, Trish, brought Evan.

By Mia's birthday the following Thursday, all twenty-four kids from Mia's class were in attendance for her animal-themed cupcake birthday party. Even Priscilla.

Pat walked into Creative Cupcakes and greeted them as if nothing negative had ever happened between them, and Andi wondered if the woman was bipolar.

"What is *she* doing here?" Rachel blurted.

"The invitation went out to Mia's entire class. Maybe this is her way of calling a truce," Andi suggested.

"She has some nerve coming in here," Kim said, narrowing her eyes. "Don't trust her, Andi. Watch her like a hawk."

Pat didn't stay but dropped her daughter off, promising to pick her up when the party was over.

"She's so happy, Andi," Jake said, glancing at Mia. "This was a great idea. And the money we brought in this week recouped the loss from the Relay for Life fundraiser."

Glowing on the inside from Jake's praise, Andi left Heather in charge of the cupcake counter and set out to help the children measure and mix ingredients without spilling sugar or getting flour everywhere, an impossible task with the number of kids on hand. Rachel and Kim did their part to help out with party games and show the kids how to decorate the cupcakes with sprinkles and plastic cake toppers.

One little boy climbed up the back corner shelving and waved his hand in front of the security camera they'd set between the fake green foliage. "Am I on TV?" he asked, reaching for the lens.

"Don't touch that," Andi said, pulling the boy down before he fell and hit his head. "You need to stay in your group."

She shook her head as she took the boy by the hand and led him back to the others. She couldn't risk having anyone get hurt, and the camera had cost Jake a small fortune, a cost they wouldn't be able to match if it was broken.

Jake's sister was the first parent to return. Evan ran up to her from the back, accompanied by Guy, and showed her his arm. "Look, Mom, I got a tattoo!"

Trish's eyes widened, and Andi quickly assured her, "It's only temporary. It washes right off with warm, soapy water."

"Evan loves your after-school program," Trish said, wiping a smudge of icing off his cheek with her thumb. "How long is the cupcake camp going to continue?"

"You want it to continue?" Andi asked, unable to hide her surprise.

The woman's face flushed. "I'm sorry I haven't been . . . nice. I dropped out of Pat's Zumba class. So did many of the others."

Andi took that to be an apology. "I think we can keep the cupcake camp running a couple times a week."

She was about to say more, but other parents had streamed through the door to pick up their children, and one of them was Pat Silverthorn. The woman, who was wearing a bright red dress, stood by the front window talking with Jake.

Andi watched Pat laugh and lean into Jake, fingering the lapel on his suit jacket. What did she think she was doing? The Zumba instructor's antics knew no bounds. Not only was she trying to put them out of business, but now she was stepping on personal turf.

But was Jake hers? Andi had shared a few noncommittal lunches and dinners with him and had immensely enjoyed every moment they had spent together over the last month. But she'd also made it clear she wouldn't rush into a new relationship.

Was Jake tired of waiting for her to make up her mind? Why didn't he move Pat's hand away from him? He couldn't be interested in a woman like that, could he? The same woman who was trying to shut down their business? Maybe if Pat dated Jake she'd leave their shop alone.

No! There was no way Pat could date Jake. It would . . . it would simply eat her alive. She cared too much for Jake.

Far too much. Her reaction the first night they met had scared her. Falling for Jake had been ... She swallowed hard and realized the truth. Falling for Jake had been love at first sight.

She couldn't allow herself to believe it until now. Her father and her friends and everyone who knew her would say she was acting impulsively again. But during her short time with Jake, she'd come to feel he might be her Mr. Right, the one she'd been meant to be with all along. And if she wanted to keep him, she would have to tell him—right after Creative Cupcakes' *official* grand opening celebration Friday night.

Chapter Nine

> Love is like swallowing hot chocolate before it
> has cooled off. It takes you by surprise at first but
> keeps you warm for a long time.
>
> —Author unknown

ANDI GLANCED OVER the business statement Jake had
left for her in the Cupcake Diary, and it didn't take a
genius to see they weren't making enough money. Hope-
fully, Rachel's idea for a big grand opening party would
pay off.

She, Rachel, and Kim had spent the entire morning
baking dozens of cupcakes. Mia and Taylor helped. Jake
promised to be at the shop by five. One of his *Astoria
Sun* coworkers, who was to write an article capturing the
highlights of the grand opening for the morning edition,

would arrive by seven. With good publicity, maybe the shop would start doing better.

Andi placed a fresh tray of spiced caramel-pear cupcakes in the display case when the door opened and in walked her father. What was he doing here?

He gave her a nod and glanced about the shop, eyeing the customers as he walked up to her. Andi was glad the counter separated them so she could brace herself against it.

"Well, I'm glad it's making money," he said, his tone more of a question than a statement.

"We have a steady flow of customers." At least that much was true.

Her father took a seat farther down the stool-lined counter, obviously planning to stay for more than a moment. He scanned the display case to his right and pointed to the spiced caramel-pear treats. "I'll take one of those."

Andi reached into the case and brought out one of the cupcakes. She placed it on a paper plate and brought it around the counter to him. When he drew out his wallet, she frowned. "Dad, please, you don't need to give me any money."

"I don't expect to get something for nothing," he said, handing her a ten-dollar bill.

Andi didn't know what to say. She never did when it came to her father. She took the money, went to the register and returned with his change.

He took a bite of the cupcake, and Andi watched for his reaction. Would he approve? He didn't indicate one way or another if he liked it or not.

"Kim doesn't know this yet," he said, lifting his gaze

to look her in the eye, "but I've sold the house, and I'm moving into a smaller place. Kim's been wanting to move out for a while, and now that the cupcake shop is generating income, she will be able to afford her own apartment."

"You sold the house?"

Andi froze and had to force herself to breathe. Where would she and Mia go if she couldn't pay her rent?

"Buying that big house was your mother's idea, not mine," her father complained. "Now that she's gone, there's no reason to stay. It's just filling up with cobwebs faster than I can knock 'em down."

"Kim and I grew up in that house," Andi said, her mind racing up the stairs to her old bedroom and all her secret hiding spots.

"I expected to have to wait a few months, but the realtor put it on the market a week ago and yesterday a friend of his called me with an offer I couldn't refuse."

Andi stared at him. "Yesterday? Why haven't you told Kim?"

Her father shrugged. "Didn't want to upset her before your grand opening tonight. Kim tends to take these things too much to heart."

"She's not the only one." Andi slumped down onto a stool beside him. "Creative Cupcakes is going to need more time before it pulls in a decent profit. We still owe for the new kitchen equipment, supplies, and half a dozen other things. What if Kim *can't* afford to get her own apartment?"

"Then she can live with you."

Andi shot up off her seat. "Dad, you can't sell the house because I—"

Kim walked through the door, and her father's look warned her not to say another word. Then after he and Kim conversed briefly, he left the shop.

Andi ground her teeth together as she refilled the napkin holders on each of the round customer tables opposite the cupcake counter. She should have told him about her eviction, begged him to keep the house. Now moving back in with her father wasn't an option. And if the grand opening didn't pull in a crowd, her sister would be as homeless as she. Then they'd all be sleeping on the floor in Rachel's one-room apartment over the garage.

Andi's anxiety compounded when a customer came in for an order she didn't have listed.

"You lost my order?" the woman before her demanded. "I need those vanilla marshmallow cupcakes for my Easter dinner party."

"Rachel, do you know anything about this?" Andi asked.

Rachel looked over from the front window, where she had hung the grand opening banner. "Yeah, I put the message in the Cupcake Diary. Fifty vanilla marshmallow cupcakes."

Andi opened the diary, and there it was:

Fifty vanilla marshmallow cupcakes for Debbie's Easter Party. Ready for pick-up Friday night.

Andi hadn't seen it. Her fault. She apologized to Debbie and packaged fifty of the same cupcakes she'd reserved for the grand opening.

After the woman had left, Andi took out the bowls and ingredients to make another batch.

"Rachel, can you please watch what you are doing?" she complained. "You're dropping confetti everywhere you go."

"Don't worry, I'll sweep," Rachel replied, smiling as she hung pink and white streamers, tissue paper cupcake replicas, and additional banners all over the shop.

"You know I want everything to be perfect for tonight's grand opening. It's critical the counters are wiped, the floor is clean, everything is in place."

"The shop has never been cleaner," Rachel told her. "You're just upset because you saw Jake getting cozy with Pat."

"They were *not* getting cozy," Andi said, slapping the dish cloth against the back counter sink.

"And it's making you irritable," Kim said, leaning in so the customers nearby couldn't hear.

"I am not irritable," Andi shot back in a fierce whisper. "Kitchen safety is rule number one. Nothing left out on the counter, all unused chairs pushed into the tables, nothing dropped on the floor."

"Nothing that can cause a fire," Rachel teased.

"Or any other kind of kitchen mishap," Kim added. "We've heard it all before."

As soon as the two police officers seated in the dining area finished their cupcakes and left, Guy emerged from the back room and stomped up to the counter. "First the shop is overrun by kids, and now because you women advertised a 'Cupcake Happy Hour,' it's becoming a local hang-out for cops."

"What's wrong with that?" Andi demanded.

"You're driving away my customers, that's what's wrong. They don't like so many cops about the place."

"And why is that?" Andi countered. "Do your customers have something to hide? If it weren't for your esteemed clientele, we wouldn't need the security camera."

"None of my 'clientele' have ever done anything to hurt your precious cupcake shop," Guy said with a growl. "Who put a bug up your butt?"

Andi braced both her arms against the edge of the counter and pressed her lips together. This was supposed to be the greatest night of their lives, the grand opening celebration of their very own business. She'd dreamed of this moment, but nothing seemed to be going as planned. Maybe they'd all been spending too much time together. They were getting on each other's nerves. Andi opened the Cupcake Diary and wrote:

> *Need to pay rent tomorrow, March 30th. (Landlord not available on 31st—Easter Sunday.) Ask Jake if there's enough money. Then save for a vacation.*

Three hours later, a photographer from Jake's newspaper and the reporter who was to write an article about the grand opening celebration showed up in the *Astoria Sun* news van. Jake told her he wished he could write the article on the shop himself, but since he was part owner, it would be considered a conflict of interest. So he had to sit back and let the other local news reporter, his friend Logan McGuire, take over.

"Logan can't be biased," Jake warned her. "He'll write up the event exactly how he sees it. But I'm not worried. The three of you have done a fabulous job preparing."

Andi took a deep breath. Jake was right. The cupcake shop had never looked better. Big white banners with the words GRAND OPENING adorned the walls. Colorful balloons floated near the ceiling. And the new CREATIVE CUPCAKES sign had arrived earlier that day to replace the temporary sheet they'd placed over the lettering from Zeke's old bar and grill.

Jake looked exquisite in his navy blue jacket and matching slacks. He smiled at her, but she couldn't help wondering if his feelings matched the depth of her own. What if he'd changed his mind and wanted their relationship to remain casual? What would he say later tonight when she told him she wanted more?

Mia ran up to her and pulled on the hem of her purple apron. "Can Taylor spend the night?"

"You'll have to ask Jake," she said. She was glad the two girls had finally worked out their differences and bonded while baking. It would make her and Jake's future relationship, if there was to be one outside of the cupcake shop, much easier.

As the customers poured into the shop, Andi, Rachel, and Kim served mini cupcakes on paper plates so everyone could sample the different flavors. The tactic had worked well at the Relay for Life fundraiser.

"I need you to start serving those cupcakes a little

faster," Andi said, glancing at Kim while taking another plate of cupcakes off the counter. "And, Rachel, your apron is coming untied."

"I like it loose," Rachel muttered under her breath. "It's easier to bend."

Andi drew her away from the crowd. "Please tie it, before you trip and fall."

"Why don't you just tie it for me so you don't have to worry about it?"

"Stop being so self-centered," Andi said in a harsh whisper. "My concern is for the shop."

"Self-centered?" Rachel retorted. "You think I'm self-centered? Ever since we started this shop, you've been temperamental, demanding, and bossy, like you and Jake are the only two who have a say in the place. You're worse than my ex-Bossinator."

Kim leaned her head in and said, "We should have the photographer take a shot of the sculpted fondant Easter bunnies on the chocolate cupcakes before they're gone. There's only a few of them left."

Ignoring Rachel, Andi asked, "Why didn't you make more?"

"I didn't have time."

"You shouldn't have taken so long to decorate each cupcake, Kim. What happens if we run out of cupcakes?"

"Then I'm sure you will decide what to do."

Andi tried to curb her emotions. "This is our dream; please smile and at least act happy."

"This was *your* dream," Kim confided. "I wanted to put my work in a real art gallery."

"Well, what's stopping you?" Andi asked. "You didn't have to be a part of this, but you always let other people make decisions for you, because you are too scared to do anything yourself."

A sharp, ear-splitting scream pierced the air, cutting off their argument. Andi turned her head to see what had happened, and in the middle of the floor, surrounded by a semi-circle of concerned onlookers, lay Pat Silverthorn.

"Someone call 911!" Jake shouted and knelt beside Pat.

Rachel took out her cell phone, and Andi rushed to the woman's side. Jake shook Pat's arm, and the woman groaned.

"I hit my head," Pat complained. "Something was on the floor, and I slipped."

Andi searched the floor and spotted the scattered cupcake wrappers. Ten of them. It was a miracle more people hadn't slipped and fallen. And after all the care in keeping the shop safe . . .

Pat sat up and directed her comments to Jake's reporter friend from the newspaper. "This place is a health hazard! Oh, my head hurts."

Within minutes sirens wailed to a stop in front of the shop, and four EMTs hurried to Pat's side.

"I'm sure I have a concussion," Pat said with a dark frown, "and it's this cupcake shop's fault."

"Stay still while we take your pulse," an EMT instructed.

"I feel dizzy," Pat said. "I think I'm going to be sick. I think you'll need the stretcher to take me to the hospital. Not only is Creative Cupcakes a sugar-infested nest of fattening, high-calorie sweeteners, but a safety hazard. I could have died slipping on the cupcake wrapper. Just wait until I call the county health department. Oh, careful how you lift me, boys."

"She's giving the performance of a lifetime," Rachel whispered.

"Will our shop's insurance cover her medical costs?" Kim asked, wringing her hands.

Andi shook her head. "I don't know. The worst of it is that she's right. If she slipped on a cupcake wrapper, then her injury is our fault."

"Too bad she didn't bite her tongue when she fell," Rachel said. "If she sues us, Creative Cupcakes will go bankrupt. Instead of a grand opening, this has been a grand disaster."

Andi looked at Jake, who looked back at her and winced, his face dark and filled with alarm. And that was more than she could take.

After all his belief in her and his continued support, she had let him down. If she'd checked the floors one more time, she could have spotted the spilled cupcake wrappers before Pat got hurt. Instead, Jake's colleague would have no choice but to do his job and write the full story of what happened in all its devastating detail.

Once the rescue unit took Pat away, the atmosphere was ruined, and the solemn crowd quickly dispersed. Jake said he wanted to talk to her after they closed up, but Andi slipped out the tattoo parlor's side door before he had the chance.

She knew it was a wimpy move, and she disliked herself for doing it, but after seeing the look on his face when Pat lay hurt on the ground, she couldn't face him. She was afraid of what he'd say, and she couldn't handle his disappointment or pity. Not now. Not from him.

She put Mia to bed and sat on the floor in the tiny cottage kitchen with her back against the refrigerator. The phone rang, and Jake left a message asking her to pick up. But she couldn't. Tears rolled down her face instead.

Creative Cupcakes had been her dream, the dream of a lifetime. If Pat sued and forced them to close, what would she do?

The phone rang three more times. When she looked at the caller ID, all three were from Jake. Then the phone stopped. She wondered if he would come over, but no one knocked at the door. Not Jake, not Rachel, not even Kim.

She'd behaved so badly. Rachel and Kim were right. She'd been stressed out, bossy, and irritable. She had no right to treat the people dearest to her heart that way. If she couldn't change Creative Cupcakes' fate, she could at least change her attitude. And she'd talk to Jake. Tomorrow.

Chapter Ten

All our dreams can come true, if we have the
courage to pursue them.

—**Walt Disney**

UNABLE TO SLEEP, Andi rose early Saturday morning and
took Mia with her to the cupcake shop. The decorations
were still up, but the multitude of uneaten cupcakes had
been put back either into the display case or into the
dozens of boxes on the back shelf. In the middle of the
marble front counter sat the Cupcake Diary.

Andi brushed her fingers across the smooth cover and
noticed someone had stuck a flyer advertising the grand
opening in the middle of the book. She opened the Cupcake Diary and found three new handwritten entries.

The first was in Kim's handwriting:

Reach for your dreams, and never let go.

Rachel had written the second:

What is life without dreams? Or good friends? We're with you, Andi, every step of the way, today, tomorrow, and the next day.

The third, no doubt, was from Guy, the tattoo artist:

Tattoo your dream to your soul, and your dream will live forever. t.

Andi smiled. Seemed like the tattoo artist would forgive them for chasing away his customers. And Rachel was right, good friends made life worthwhile, even when the days became dark. Look at the adventure they had had! And her little sister, Kim, younger in years, but older in her heart.

"Mia, go over to the window and turn the CLOSED sign to OPEN."

"Okay, Mom."

The press could write a bad article, the county could try to shut the shop down, and the Zumba lady might be a sworn enemy forever, but she wouldn't quit.

Today was a brand-new day.

AN HOUR LATER, Rachel and Kim walked through the door of the kitchen, and without a word, they both wrapped Andi in a group hug.

"I was wrong to take the lead and be so bossy," Andi said, shifting her gaze from Rachel to Kim. "I was so worried and driven to succeed I forgot what real success is all about—having people care about you who you care about in return." She gave each of them a tight squeeze. "I promise from now on, we will be equal partners in this shop."

"And we're sorry about the mean things we said, too," Kim said, her voice low. "You're the one who is always after us about kitchen safety, and we overlooked seeing these on the floor."

Kim bent down, picked up one of the cupcake wrappers from the night before, and frowned. "This isn't our cupcake wrapper."

"What?" Andi held her breath as she and Rachel hurried over to see for themselves.

Kim pointed to the outside of the wrapper. "This is a thin pink wrapper like the ones they sell in the supermarket. Ours have the thicker, reinforced sides that Andi insisted on."

"Then where did they come from?" Andi asked. She feared she already knew the answer.

"A lady took them out of her purse and threw them on the ground like this," Mia said, mimicking the gesture. She twirled around and flicked her hands as if tossing Frisbees.

"What lady, Mia?" Andi pressed.

Rachel put her hands on her hips. "I'll give you one guess."

"Pat?"

"Yup. She guessed it," Mia said, bouncing up and down. "Priscilla said her mom's name is Pat."

Andi shook her head. "Even if it's true, we have no proof."

"Yes, we do," Kim said and pointed up toward the security camera hidden among the fake floral greenery.

OFFICER LOCKWELL CAME in on his coffee break and helped them review the surveillance video.

"There," he said, stopping the images scrolling across the screen. "The woman took them from her purse, scattered them all over the floor while you three were arguing, and after a quick look to see if anyone was watching, faked her fall to the floor."

"Unbelievable!" Andi exclaimed. But the proof was right in front of her eyes.

Rachel shook her head. "Can we have her arrested?"

"Sorry," Officer Lockwell said. "The police don't get involved in civil cases."

"Have you talked to Jake?" Kim asked. "Maybe he can stop his newspaper from writing the story from Pat's point of view and present the truth before it's too late."

The shop's door opened, and Andi looked up expectantly, hoping it was Jake. No such luck. It was her father.

He locked his gaze on her and furrowed his brow. "You've really done it this time. The whole town is talking about what happened last night. I tried to tell you not to pursue this silly notion you had to open a cupcake shop, but you—"

"Stop!" Kim said, cutting him off.

Andi gave her a surprised look. So did their father.

"You should be proud of Andi," Kim told him. "She had the courage to do what most people only dream about—she opened her own business. There's nothing silly about that."

Andi silently thanked her sister.

Their father grunted. "I don't see any customers in here except me. How's that for success?"

Andi avoided his gaze and called Jake on the phone. "He's not answering." Was this payback for her not answering his calls the night before? "We'll have to take the video straight to him at his office."

WITH THE PROOF to restore Creative Cupcakes' reputation, Andi, Rachel, and Kim left Mia and her grandfather to watch over the shop and made a mad dash across town to the offices of the *Astoria Sun*.

"We need to see Jake Hartman," Andi told the assistant at the front desk.

"Mr. Hartman isn't available right now," the assistant informed her. "If you have a news tip, I can give you his email address, and he can contact you."

"My news tip can't wait," Andi said, staring at the massive logo of the newspaper on the wall behind her. "Where is his desk?"

"I'm sorry, but I can't give out that information."

"But I'm his girlfriend."

The assistant's head lurched back in surprise, and she squinted down the bridge of her nose, as if assessing her.

"Girlfriend? I didn't think the man ever dated."

A guy in his early sixties came around the corner and handed the assistant a stack of files. "Is there a problem?"

The assistant whispered, "They want to see Jake."

Rachel leaned over the front desk and stuck her curly red head in his face. "We're from Creative Cupcakes."

"I'm the senior editor," the man informed them. "How can I help you?"

"There's been a new development," Andi said in a rush. "Your newspaper can't print the article on the cupcake shop until you have all the facts."

"We already did," he said. "It came out this morning."

Andi shot a worried look toward Rachel and Kim and then turned back to him. "Can we still see Jake?"

"He's not here. He went with Logan McGuire and the photographer to the cupcake shop to meet *you*."

"He's at Creative Cupcakes?"

"With Pat Silverthorn. She's home from the hospital and issuing a public statement."

Rachel scowled. "How dare she!"

Kim's jaw dropped.

Andi bit her lip, her imagination running wild with the prospect of Pat recapping her scandalized version to the media. Taking out her cell phone, she called the shop. When there was no answer, she called the tattoo artist.

"Guy, can I ask a favor?"

"Where are you?" he exclaimed. "The Zumba lady is here with Jake, a reporter, a photographer, and everything is turning into chaos."

"We'll be there in fifteen minutes. Can you serve the news crew cupcakes until we get there?"

"What about the others?" Guy asked.

Andi hesitated. "Others?"

"The *Astoria Sun* van has drawn a crowd of on-lookers."

Andi groaned. "There are plenty of cupcakes left from last night. Serve as many as you can."

WHEN ANDI, RACHEL, and Kim arrived back at the shop, there were more people gathered around Creative Cupcakes than at their grand opening event the night before.

Guy stood on the sidewalk serving cupcakes to the crowd, with Mia, half his height, as his helper. Both wore the purple bakery aprons, the tattoo artist's over his black T-shirt and jeans, Mia's flowing down to her toes like a dress. Andi's father looked out the shop window, his eyes wide. Jake stood on the sidewalk with Logan McGuire, who appeared to be interviewing Pat Silverthorn.

Andi drew closer.

"Don't do anything impulsive," Rachel warned.

"Think before you speak," Kim added. "Take your time, don't rush."

Andi didn't rush; she just always did everything at a faster, more accelerated pace than everyone else. If her decisions got her into trouble in the past, it was because she didn't really know what she wanted. Now she did. She wanted to save her business ... and she wanted a relationship with Jake.

"I think these are the other three owners coming in now," said Logan McGuire, directing his comment to the photographer.

Jake turned his head and looked straight at her. "I've been to your house and all over looking for you."

Andi glanced at the flash of the camera which took their picture. "You have?"

"My sister witnessed Pat Silverthorn's deliberate fall last night and came and told me right away. It wasn't Creative Cupcakes' fault."

"Why is she here?" Andi asked and motioned to Pat, whose eyes were red and swollen.

"I'm sorry, Andi," Pat said, her usual smug expression absent from her face. "My mother died from a lifetime of unhealthy eating habits. The last thing she ate was a big sugary cupcake. I . . . I'm sorry I took out my anger on your shop and for my behavior last night. What I did was very wrong."

"I would say so." Rachel glared at her. "You think you can get off the hook for what you did by apologizing? Is that what this is all about? Andi, we should sue *her*!"

"No," Andi said, setting her jaw. "We're not going to sue."

"Why not?" Rachel demanded.

"Because that's not who we are."

Rachel was quiet a moment and then said, "You're right."

Pat bowed her head in shame. "I haven't handled my mother's death very well. She was all I had, and I miss her."

Andi missed Jake. She watched him walk toward the open side door of the van and when he returned he handed her an enormous bouquet of—yellow lilies! She brought them to her nose and closed her eyes as she breathed in their strong sweet scent. Then Jake showed her the article the *Astoria Sun* had printed: "Zumba Instructor Caught Staging Cupcake Disaster."

"CREATIVE CUPCAKES HAS been selling like crazy," Jake said, putting his arm around her shoulders and giving her a squeeze. "We can hardly serve fast enough."

"All these people are here to buy cupcakes?" Andi asked, glancing around.

Mia turned toward her, grinning, and pointed to the money threatening to spill out of her overstuffed apron pocket.

"Let's open the door," Andi announced.

Rachel and Kim hurried after her as they ran to grab their aprons, wash their hands, and pull on disposable food handler's gloves. Andi began to take orders and noticed her father pulling gloves on his hands as well.

He turned, and she caught his eye. What did he think he was doing?

Her father gave her a wary look. "Andi, you're going to need more cupcakes."

As he served the next customer, she broke into a smile. "Thanks, Dad."

Pat Silverthorn also offered to help, which put an even larger twist on the current news story.

Logan McGuire tasted one of their cupcakes and asked, "What do you think of the new French bakery opening up on the other side of town?"

Andi gave him a broad grin. "As long as we get along, everything will be fine."

Rachel took a box from under the counter and pulled out a large gold-plated cake knife with CREATIVE CUP-CAKES engraved on the handle. "A symbol of our success."

"The victory cupcake cutter!" Andi said, waving it high in the air.

"Makes me believe we can do almost anything," Rachel confided and began to sing a sultry rendition of Israel Kamakawiwoʻole's version of the song classic "Somewhere Over the Rainbow." She finished with the line "Dreams really do come true."

Andi clapped and laughed. Then Kim pulled her T-shirt down over her left shoulder to reveal a tattoo of a flying squirrel.

"Kim, you didn't!"

"I did," Kim said proudly.

"Did what?" their father asked.

Kim slid her shirt back into place and grinned. "Nothing, Dad. Just talking about the freedom to fly with your dreams."

"Did Dad tell you about the house?" Andi asked.

"Yeah, so . . . is it all right if I stay with you until I find my own apartment?"

Andi hesitated, and as fate would have it, Rachel pointed to a late arrival waiting by the cupcake counter. "It's your landlord."

Andi looked over at Jake. "Is there enough money?"

Jake opened the cash register, pulled out several large bills, and directed his attention to her landlord. "How much does she owe you?"

"Eight hundred for last month. Another eight hundred if she wants to keep the cottage," the man informed him.

Jake shot Andi a questioning gaze, and she nodded.

"Yes, I want to stay."

"Good luck," the landlord told her, taking the money. Then he hesitated, turned back, and pointed at the triple chocolate cupcakes inside the display case. "I'll take one of those."

BY THE END of the day, Creative Cupcakes had sold more than they had all month, and after a late-night dinner, Jake took Andi out on the covered platform at the end of the pier.

Dim lights cast a golden glow over the waterfront docks, and sea lions barked harmoniously back and forth to each other from beneath the pilings. The air was warmer than usual for early spring, the sky clear and sprinkled with stars.

"I'm sorry I ran out and didn't return your calls," Andi said, sitting on the bench beside him. "When Pat slipped and fell, I saw your face, and after promising to make Creative Cupcakes a success, I couldn't stand to see you disappointed."

Jake took her hand in his. "I wasn't disappointed in you. I was disappointed *for* you."

"You cringed."

"Of course I cringed. Pat came up to me at Mia's birthday party and wanted to know if the newspaper was going to cover the grand opening. I regret to say I told her yes. Then when she fell, I knew my newspaper would have to print the story, and I knew how much it would hurt you. I couldn't stand to see you hurt, Andi. I cringed because I didn't want to fail *you*."

"Someone as sweet as you could never fail me, Jake."

He took her in his arms and gazed directly into her eyes. "You haven't found anything about me to scare you off yet?"

Andi shook her head, her face inches away from his. "No, not yet."

"Maybe it's the way I kiss," he teased, his breath warm against her skin. "It could be detestable."

There was no way Jake's kiss could be detestable, but since he was joking, she decided to play along.

"Yes, it could be."

He brushed a strand of her long blond hair back behind her ear and tilted her chin up. "Only one way to find out."

"I suppose." Andi caught her breath, the anticipation nearly killing her.

Then Jake brushed his mouth across hers in a tender, whisper-soft kiss that made her heart soar and her insides sing a melodious sweet-scented love song.

"Scared?" he asked, drawing back.

Andi smiled and shook her head. "Not yet. Keep trying."

Jake lowered his mouth to kiss her again, then halted halfway and grinned. "Does this mean we can finally go on a real date?"

"What if I told you I'd love to go on as many dates with you as I can?"

"What if I told you," he said, his voice husky as he played along, "I'd like every date on the calendar?"

"I'd say they're yours," Andi said, locking her gaze with his, "but you know we do have a cupcake shop to run."

"Yes, *we* do," he agreed and tipped his mouth toward hers again with all the tenderness of a white cloud cupcake with sweet heavenly frosting.

Recipe for
PAUL HANSON'S CARROT CAKE

From the author's great-uncle, Paul Hanson

In a large bowl, combine the dry ingredients:

2 cups sifted flour

1 tsp. baking powder

1 tsp. baking soda

1 tsp. cinnamon

1/4 tsp. salt

In another bowl mix:

1 1/2 cups salad oil

2 cups sugar

Add 4 beaten eggs, one at a time, and mix well after adding each egg. Gradually fold in 2 cups of finely grated carrots. Add dry ingredients. Mix well.

Bake 50 to 60 minutes at 350° (less time for cupcakes).

Icing:

1/2 cup butter or margarine

1 (8oz.) pkg. cream cheese

Beat until light and fluffy, gradually adding:

3 3/4 cup powdered sugar

1 tsp. vanilla

(1 cup chopped pecans - optional)

*Keep reading for a sneak peek at the next
two books in* The Cupcake Diaries,

RECIPE FOR LOVE

and

TASTE OF ROMANCE,

*available from Avon Impulse
May 14, 2013, and May 21, 2013!*

An Excerpt from

THE CUPCAKE DIARIES: RECIPE FOR LOVE

Life is uncertain. Eat dessert first.

—Ernestine Ulmer

RACHEL PUSHED THROUGH the double doors of the kitchen, took one look at the masked man at the counter, and dropped the fresh baked tray of cupcakes on the floor.

Did he plan to rob Creative Cupcakes, demand she hand over the money from the cash register? Her eyes darted around the frilly pink-and-white shop. The loud clang of the metal bakery pan hitting the tile had caused several customers sitting at the tables to glance in her direction. Would the masked man threaten the other people as well? How could she protect them?

She stepped over the white frosted chocolate mess by her feet, tried to judge the distance to the telephone on the wall, and turned her attention back to the masked man before her. Maybe he wasn't a robber but someone dressed for a costume party or play. The man with the black masquerade mask covering the upper half of his face also wore a black cape.

"If this is a hold-up, you picked the wrong place, Zorro." She tossed her fiery red curls over her shoulder with false bravado and laid a protective hand across the old bell-ringing register. "We don't have any money."

His hazel eyes sparkled through the holes in the mask, and he flashed her a disarming smile. "Maybe I can help with that."

He turned his hand to show an empty palm, and relief flooded over her. No gun. Then he closed his fingers and swung his fist around in the air three times. When he opened his palm again, he held a quarter, which he tossed in her direction.

Rachel caught the coin and laughed. "You're a magician."

"Mike the Magnificent," he said, extending his cape wide with one arm and taking a bow. "I'm here for the Lockwell party."

Rachel pointed to the door leading to the back party room. The space had originally been a tattoo shop, but the tattoo artist relocated to the rental next door. "The Lockwells aren't here yet. The party doesn't start until three."

"I came early to set up before the kids arrive," Mike told her. "Can't have them discovering my secrets."

"No, I guess not," Rachel agreed. "If they did, Mike the magician might not be so magnificent."

"Magnificence is hard to maintain." His lips twitched, as if suppressing a grin. "Are you Andi?"

She shook her head. "Rachel, Creative Cupcakes' stupendous co-owner, baker, and promoter."

This time a grin did escape his mouth, which led her to notice his strong, masculine jawline.

"Tell me, Rachel, what is it that makes you so stupendous?"

She gave him her most flirtatious smile. "Sorry, I can't reveal my secrets, either."

"Afraid if I found out the truth I might not think you're so impressively great?"

Rachel froze, fearing Mike the magician might be a mind reader as well. Careful to keep her smile intact, she forced herself to laugh off his comment.

"I just don't think it's nice to brag," she responded playfully.

"Chicken," he taunted in an equally playful tone as he made his way toward the party room door.

Despite the uneasy feeling he'd discovered more about her in three minutes than most men did in three years, she wished he'd stayed to chat a few minutes more.

Andi Burke, wearing one of the new, hot-pink Creative Cupcakes bibbed aprons, came in from the kitchen and stared at the cupcake mess on the floor. "What happened here?"

"Zorro came in, gave me a panic attack, and the tray slipped out of my hands." Rachel grabbed a couple of paper towels and squatted down to scoop up the crumpled cake and splattered frosting before her OCD kitchen safety friend could comment further. "Don't worry, I'll take care of the mess."

"I should have told you Officer Lockwell hired a magician for his daughter's birthday party." Andi bent to help her, and when they stood back up, she asked, "Did you speak to Mike?"

Rachel nodded, her gaze on the connecting door to the party room as it opened, and Mike reappeared. Tipping his head as he strolled past them, he said, "Good afternoon, ladies."

Mike went out the front door and Rachel hurried around the display case of cupcakes and crossed over to the shop's square, six-foot-high, street-side window. She leaned her head toward the glass and watched him take four three-by-three-foot black painted boxes out of the back of a van.

"You should go after him," Andi teased, her voice filled with amusement. "He's very handsome."

"How can you tell?" Rachel drew away from the window, afraid Mike might catch her spying on him. "He's got a black mask covering the upper half of his face. He could have sunken eyes, shaved eyebrows, and facial tattoos."

Andi laughed. "He doesn't, and I know you like guys with dark hair. He's not as tall as my Jake, but he's still got a great build."

"Better not let Jake hear you say that," Rachel retorted. "And how do you know he has a great build? The guy's wrapped in a cape."

"I've seen him before," Andi said. "Without the cape."

"Where?"

"His photo was in the newspaper two weeks ago," Andi confided. "The senior editor at the *Astoria Sun* assigned Jake to write an article on Mike Palmer's set models."

"What are you talking about?"

"Mike Palmer created the miniature model replica of the medieval city of Hilltop for the movie *Battle for Warrior Mountain* and worked on set pieces for *The Goonies*, *Kindergarten Cop*, and many of the other movies filmed around Astoria. His structural designs are so intricate that when the camera zooms in close, it looks real."

Mike returned through the front door, wheeling in the black boxes on an orange dolly. Rachel caught her breath as he looked her way before proceeding toward the party room with his equipment. Did the masked man find her as intriguing as she found him?

Andi's younger sister, Kim, came in from the kitchen with a large tray of red velvet cupcakes with cherry cream cheese frosting. The three of them together, with Andi's boyfriend, Jake Hartman, as their financial partner, had managed to open Creative Cupcakes a month and a half earlier.

"Who's he?" Kim asked. She placed the cupcakes on the marble counter and pointed toward the billowing black cape of the magician.

"Mike the Magnificent," Rachel said, dreamily.

OFFICER IAN LOCKWELL, his wife, son, and daughter entered the shop a short while later. The first time Rachel had met him, he'd written her a parking ticket. Since then, he had helped chase off a group of fanatical Zumba dancers who were trying to shut down Creative Cupcakes and had become one of their biggest supporters. Both were good reasons for her to reverse her original harsh feelings toward the blond, square-jawed man.

"Happy Birthday, Caitlin," Rachel greeted his six-year-old daughter. "Ready for the magic show?"

"I hope he pulls a rabbit out of his hat," Caitlin said, her eyes sparkling. "I asked for a rabbit for my birthday."

"She wanted one last month for Easter," Officer Lockwell confided. "But I told her the bunnies were busy delivering eggs."

"There are always more rabbits in April," Andi told Caitlin and winked conspiratorially at her father. "Isn't there?"

Officer Lockwell shifted his gaze to the ceiling.

"Should we go to the party room?" Rachel asked, leading the way.

"Here's two more," Jake Hartman said, ushering his little girl, Taylor, and Andi's daughter, Mia, into the shop. Both five-year-olds attended the same kindergarten class as Caitlin at Astor Elementary.

Andi stepped forward and gave Jake a kiss before he had to head back to work at the newspaper office.

"Is he a real magician, Mom?" Mia asked Andi, hugging her legs as Mike the Magnificent came out to welcome them.

"As real as they get," Andi assured her.

Rachel exchanged a look with Andi above Mia's head and smiled. "I wonder if he needs an assistant."

IN THE PRIVACY of the kitchen, Andi pulled the pink bandana off Rachel's hair. "That's better. Now primp your curls."

"And don't forget to swing your hips as you serve the cupcakes," Kim added. "Maybe Magic Mike will wave his wand and whisk you under his cape for a kiss."

"I can hope," Rachel said. "I haven't had a date in two weeks."

"Is that a new record?" Andi teased.

"Almost."

"Maybe if you kept one guy around long enough, you wouldn't have to worry about finding a date," Kim said, arching one of her delicate dark brows.

"Oh, no!" Rachel shook her head. "Rule number one. *Never* date the same man three times in a row. First dates are fabulous, second dates fun, but third dates? That's when guys start to think they freaking know you, and the relationship fails. Better to stick with two dates and forget the rest."

"Jake and I continue to have fun," Andi argued.

"That's because you and Jake are made for each other." Rachel picked up the tray of cupcakes they'd decorated to look like white rabbits peeking out from chocolate top hats. "And so far, I haven't met any man who looks at me the way he looks at you. If I *did*," she said, pausing to make sure her friend got the hint, "I'd marry him."

Andi pushed a strand of her long, dark blond hair behind her ear and blushed. "Maybe Mike will be your man."

"Maybe," Rachel conceded and smiled. "But every relationship starts with a first date."

WHEN RACHEL ENTERED the room, Mike was in the middle of performing a card trick. She scanned the faces of the two dozen kids sitting at the long, rectangular tables covered with pink partyware and colorful birthday presents. Mike did a good job of holding their attention. They sat in wide-eyed fascination. Not one of them noticed her as she distributed the cupcakes to each place setting.

Next, Mike the Magnificent showed the audience the inside of his empty black top hat. Placing the hat rightside up on one of his black boxes, he waved his wand over the top and quickly flipped the hat upside down again. Rachel smiled as he invited the birthday girl up to the hat. The six-year-old reached her hand in and pulled out a fake toy bunny with big, white floppy ears.

Caitlin looked at Mike, her eyes betraying her disappointment, then mumbled, "Thanks."

"Were you hoping for a real rabbit?" Mike asked her.

Caitlin nodded.

"Let's try that again." Mike told Caitlin to put the stuffed bunny back into the hat. Then he turned the hat over and placed it down on the black box again. He waved the wand. This time when he turned the hat over a live rabbit with big, white floppy ears poked its head up over the top of the rim.

Caitlin let out an excited squeal, and Rachel laughed. Mike the Magnificent was good with the kids and a good magician. How did he do it? She stared at the box and the black hat and couldn't tell how he'd been able to make the switch.

Dodging a couple of the strings that hung down from the balloons bobbing against the ceiling, she moved closer.

"Just the person I was looking for," Mike said, catching her eye. "Rachel, could you come up here for a moment?"

"Certainly." Rachel gave him a wide smile and moved to his side. "What would you like me to do?"

"Get in the box."

Rachel glanced at the large horizontal black box resting upon two sawhorses at the front of the room. It looked eerily like a coffin.

"And take off your shoes," he added under his breath.

Rachel stepped out of her pink pumps, and when Mike moved aside the black curtain covering the box, she slid inside.

"How about a pillow?" Mike asked.

"A pillow would be nice," she said.

His large, warm hand cupped the back of her head as he placed the white cushion beneath her, and his gaze locked with hers. "Are you married?"

Rachel's eyes widened. "No."

"Have a steady boyfriend?"

Rachel shook her head.

"Good," Mike said and grinned at the audience. "I won't have to worry about anyone coming after me if something goes wrong."

"What do you mean, '*if something goes wrong*'?" she demanded.

He held up a carpenter's saw with a very large, jagged blade, and the kids in the audience giggled with delight.

"He's going to saw her in half!" Mia exclaimed. "I don't think my mommy will like that. How will Rachel help my mom bake cupcakes?"

"Saw me in half?" Rachel gasped and stared up at Mike. How did this trick work? He wasn't really going to come near her with that saw, was he? "I . . . uh . . . have a slight fear of blades. If I get hurt, do you have a girlfriend or wife I can complain to?"

Mike grinned. "No wife. But if you survive, maybe I'll marry you."

The young audience edged forward in anticipation probably wondering if they'd see blood or hear her scream.

Rachel had done some pretty crazy things in the past to get a date, but this ridiculous stunt had to top them all. "I really am afraid of blades," she said, her voice raised to a high-pitched squeak.

"Don't worry; I've only killed two people in the past," Mike reassured her, then leaned down to whisper in her ear, "Roll to your side and curl up in a ball."

Rachel did as she was told and faced the audience. There was more room in the box than she'd first supposed. Mike made a few quick adjustments, and an inside board slid up against her feet. Then he raised the shark-toothed blade above her and began to saw the outside of the box in two.

The box rattled, and the fresh sawdust made her sneeze, making the kids laugh.

"Does it hurt?" Caitlin asked.

"Not yet," Rachel admitted.

"Here we go," Mike announced.

Rachel closed her eyes, and memories of her uncle filled her mind. Distracted, he'd slipped while working a circular saw and cut off three of his fingers. Blood spurt in every direction. She'd been seven and stood by his side when it happened.

Everyone in the room shouted as Mike pulled the black boxes apart. Rachel frowned. She didn't feel any different.

"Rachel, are you alive?" Mia called out.

"Yes, I'm still here."

Jake's daughter, Taylor, pointed. "Her feet are sticking out of the other half of the box."

"How do you know those feet are mine?" Rachel challenged, knowing her bare toes were still curled beneath her.

Caitlin laughed. "They are wearing your pink shoes."

Rachel craned her head around to see the other half of the black box several feet away. The two flesh-colored, lifelike feet sticking out of the end wore her pink pumps.

"How 'bout we put Rachel back together?" Mike suggested.

The kids clapped and cheered.

Moving the two boxes back together, Mike motioned for her to slide out of the first wooden compartment. Then he removed the set of fake feet out of the second compartment and gave her back her pink pumps. When she'd slipped them on, he took her hand and led her in front of the audience.

"She's back together again!" Mia exclaimed.

"Take a bow," Mike told her. "You've earned it"

"I survived." Rachel tilted her head and gave the masked magician a questioning look to remind him of his earlier words. But he didn't ask her to marry him.

He didn't even ask her for a date.

Disappointed, Rachel left the party and headed back to the kitchen, where Andi and Kim waited for a progress report.

"Does he like you?" Andi asked.

"Oh, yes," Rachel said and swallowed the knot in the back of her throat. "He called me a 'good sport.'"

An Excerpt from

THE CUPCAKE DIARIES: TASTE OF ROMANCE

> All I really need is love, but a little chocolate now
> and then doesn't hurt!
>
> **—Charles Schulz**

Focus, Kim reprimanded herself. *Keep to the task at hand and stop eavesdropping on other people's conversations.*

But she didn't need to hear the crack of the teenage boy's heart to feel his pain. Or to remember the last time she'd heard the wretched words *"I'm leaving"* spoken to her.

She tried to ignore the couple as she picked up the pastry bag filled with pink icing and continued to decorate the tops of the strawberry preserve cupcakes.

However, the discussion between the high school boy and what she assumed to be his girlfriend kept her attentive.

"When will I see you again?" the boy asked.

Kim glanced toward them, leaned closer, and held her breath.

"I don't know," the girl replied.

The soft lilt in her accent thrust the familiarity of the conversation even deeper into Kim's soul.

"I'll be going to the university for two years," the girl continued. "Maybe we meet again after."

Not likely. Kim shook her head, and the bottom of her stomach locked down tight. From past experience, she knew once the school year was over in June, most foreign students went home, never to return.

And left many broken hearts in their wake.

"Two years is a long time," the boy said.

Forever was even longer. Kim drew in a deep breath, as the unmistakable catch in the poor boy's voice replayed again and again in her mind. And her heart.

How long were they going to stand there and torment her and remind her of her parting four years earlier with Gavin, the Irish student she'd dated through college? Dropping the bag of icing on the Creative Cupcakes counter, she moved toward them.

"Can I help you?" Kim asked, pulling on a new pair of food handler's gloves.

"I'll have the white chocolate macadamia," the girl said, pointing to the cupcake she wanted in the glass display case.

The boy dug his hands into his pockets, counted the

meager change he'd managed to withdraw, and turned five shades of red.

"None for me." His Adam's apple bobbed as he swallowed. "How much for hers?"

"You have to have one, too," the girl protested. "It's your birthday."

Kim looked at his lost-for-words expression and took pity on him. "If today is your birthday, the cupcakes are free," she said. "For both you and your guest."

The teenager's face brightened. "Really?"

Kim nodded and removed the cupcakes the two lovebirds wanted from the display case. She even put a birthday candle on one of them, a heart on the other. Maybe the girl would come back for him, or he would fly to Ireland for her. *Maybe.*

Her eyes stung, and she squeezed them shut for a brief second. When she opened them again, she set her jaw. Enough was enough. Now that they had their cupcakes she could escape back into her work and forget about romance and relationships and every regrettable moment she'd ever wasted on love.

She didn't need it. Not like her older sister, Andi, who recently lost her heart to Jake Hartman, their Creative Cupcakes financier and news reporter for the *Astoria Sun.* Or like her other co-owner friend, Rachel, who just gotten engaged to Mike Palmer, a miniature model maker for movies who also doubled as the driver of their Cupcake Mobile.

All she needed was to dive deep into her desire to put paint on canvas. She glanced at the walls of the cupcake shop, adorned with her scenic oil, acrylic, and watercolor paintings. Maybe if she worked hard enough, she'd have the money to open her own art gallery, and she wouldn't need to decorate cupcakes anymore.

But for now, she needed to serve the next customer. *Where was Rachel?*

"Hi, Kim." Officer Ian Lockwell, one of their biggest supporters, sat on one of the stools lining the marble cupcake counter. "I'm wondering if you have the back party room available on June twenty-seventh?"

Kim reached under the counter and pulled out the three-ring binder she, Andi, and Rachel had dubbed the Cupcake Diary to keep track of all things cupcake related. Looking at the calendar, she said, "Yes, the date is open. What's the occasion?"

"My wife and I have been married almost fifteen years," the big square-jawed cop told her. "We're planning on renewing our vows on our anniversary and need a place to celebrate with friends and family."

"No better place to celebrate love than Creative Cupcakes," Kim assured him, glancing around at all the couples in the shop. "I'll put you on the schedule."

Next, the door opened and a stream of romance writers filed in for their weekly meeting. Kim pressed her lips together. The group intimidated her with their watchful eyes and poised pens. They scribbled in their notebooks whenever she walked by as if writing down her every move, and she didn't want to give them any useful fodder. She hoped Rachel could take their orders, if she could find her.

"Rachel?"

No answer, but the phone rang—a welcome distraction. She picked up and said, "Creative Cupcakes, this is Kim."

"What are you doing there? I thought you were going to take time off."

Kim pushed into the privacy of the kitchen, glad it was her sister, Andi, and not another customer despite the impending lecture tone. "I still have several dozen cupcakes to decorate."

"Isn't Rachel there with you?"

The door of the walk-in pantry burst open, and Rachel Donovan and her fiancé, Mike Palmer, emerged, wrapped in each other's arms, laughing and grinning.

Kim rolled her eyes. "Yes, Rachel's here."

Rachel extracted herself from Mike's embrace and mouthed the word "Sorry."

But Kim knew she wasn't. Rachel had been in her own red-headed happy bubble ever since macho, dark-haired Mike the Magnificent had proposed two weeks earlier.

"I'll be in for my shift as soon as I get Mia off to afternoon kindergarten," Andi continued, "and the shop's way ahead in sales. There's no reason you can't take a break. Ever since you broke up with Gavin, you've become a workaholic."

Kim sucked in her breath at the mention of his name. Only Andi dared to ever bring him up.

"Gavin has nothing to do with my work."

"You never date."

"I'm concentrating on my career."

"It's been years since you've been out with anyone. You need to slow down, take time to smell the roses."

"Smell the roses?" Kim gasped. "Are you *serious*?"

"Go on an adventure," Andi amended.

"Working is an adventure."

"You used to dream of a different kind of adventure," Andi said, lowering her voice. "The kind that requires a passport."

Kim wished she'd never picked up the phone. Just because her sister had her life put back together didn't mean she had the right to tell her how to live.

"Painting cupcakes and canvas is the only adventure I need right now. I promised Dad I'd have the money to pay him for my new easel by the end of the week."

"Dad doesn't care about the money, but he does care about you. He asked me to call."

"He did?" Kim stopped in front of the sink and rubbed her temples with her fingertips. Her sister was known to overreact, but their dad? He didn't voice concern unless it was legitimate.

With the phone to her ear, she returned to the front counter of the couple-filled cupcake shop, her heart screaming louder and louder with each consecutive beat.

They were *everywhere*. By the window, at the tables, next to the display case. Couples, couples, couples. Everyone had a partner, had someone.

Almost everyone.

Instead of Goonies Day, the celebration for the 1985 release date of *The Goonies* movie filmed in Astoria, she would have thought the calendar had been flipped back to Valentine's Day at Creative Cupcakes. And in her opinion, one Valentine's Day a year was more than enough.

She reached a hand into the pocket of her pink apron and clenched the golden wings she received on her first airplane flight as a child. The pin never left her side and like the flying squirrel tattooed on her shoulder, reminded her of her dream to fly, if not to another land, then at least to the farthest reaches of her imagination.

Where her heart would be free.

Okay, maybe she *did* spend too much time at the cupcake shop. "Tell Dad not to worry," Kim said into the phone. "Tell him . . . I'm taking the afternoon off."

"Promise?" Andi persisted.

Oh, yeah. Tearing off her apron, she turned around and threw it over Rachel's and Mike's heads. "I'm heading out the door now."

FIVE MINUTES LATER, Kim stood outside the Astoria cupcake shop on Marine Drive, wondering which direction to go. The tattoo parlor was to her left, a boutique to her right, and the waterfront walk beneath the giant arching framework of the Astoria–Megler Bridge stretched straight in front.

Turning her back on it all, she decided to take a new path and soon discovered an open wrought iron gate along Bond Road, the side entrance to Astoria's new community park. Hadn't her sister told her to smell the roses?

Kim walked through the gate toward the large circle of white rosebushes and began to count off each flower as she leaned in to fill her lungs with their strong, fragrant scent. "One, two, three . . ."

After smelling seventeen, she moved toward the yellows. "Eighteen, nineteen, twenty . . ."

Past the gazebo she found red roses, orange roses, and a vast variety of purple and pinks. "Forty-six, forty-seven, forty-eight . . ."

Her artist's eye took in the palette of color, and imagining the scene on canvas, she wished she'd brought along her paints and brushes. "Sixty-two, sixty-three, sixty-four . . ."

Andi had been right. The sweet, perfumed scent of the roses did seem to ease her tension and help block out all thoughts of romance. Even if the rose was a notorious symbol of *love*. And the flower that garnished the most sales over *romantic* holidays. With petals used for flower girl baskets at *weddings*.

Who needed romance anyway? Not her.

She bent to smell the next group of flowers and noticed a tall, blond man with work gloves carrying a potted rosebush past the ivy trellis. As his gaze caught hers, he appeared to pause. Then he smiled.

Kim smiled back and moved toward the next rose.

"Can I help you?" the gardener asked, walking over.

Oh, *no*. He had a foreign accent, Scandinavian, like some of the locals whose ancestors first inhabited the area. And she had an acute weakness for foreign accents.

"I think I need to do this myself," Kim replied. "My goal is to smell a hundred roses."

"Why a hundred?"

"That's the number of things on my to-do list. I thought stopping to smell one rose per task might balance out my life."

"Interesting concept." The attractive gardener appeared to suppress a grin. "How many more do you have to go?"

"I'm at sixty-seven."

"I didn't mean to interrupt." He set the rosebush down, took off a glove, and extended his hand. "I'm Nathaniel Sjölander."

"Kimberly Burke," she said, accepting the handshake. His hand, much larger than her own, surrounded her with warmth.

"I have to load a couple dozen roses into my truck for the Portland Rose Festival tomorrow, but by all means—keep sniffing."

Kim pulled rose number sixty-eight toward her, a yellow flower as buttery and delicately layered as a . . . freshly baked croissant. Hunger sprang to life inside her empty stomach, and she realized she'd been so busy working, she'd forgotten to eat lunch.

She watched Nathaniel Sjölander move between the potted plants. Was he single? Would someone like him be interested in her? Maybe ask her to dinner? And why *hadn't* she dated anyone in the last few years? She could argue that good-looking single men were hard to come by, but the truth was, she just hadn't taken the initiative to find one.

Nathaniel made several trips back and forth between the greenhouse and the gate, his gaze sliding toward her again and again. *Oh, yes!* He was definitely interested. Her pulse quickened as he approached her a second time.

"I think you missed a few." Nathaniel pulled a cut bouquet of red roses from behind his back and presented them to her.

"Thank you." She hugged the flowers against her chest and lifted her gaze from the Sjölander's Garden Nursery business logo embroidered on his tan workshirt to his warm, kind . . . *blue* eyes.

Oh, man, why did they have to be blue? Blue was her favorite color. She could get lost in blue. Especially *his* blue, a blend of sparkling azure with a hint of sea green. They reminded her of the ripples in the water where the Columbia River met the Pacific Ocean just outside Astoria.

"Sjölander. Is that Finnish?" she asked.

"Swedish. Most of my family resides in Sweden, with the exception of my brother and a few cousins."

His name was incredibly familiar. Where had she come across the name Sjölander before? The Cupcake Diary!

"I'm co-owner of Creative Cupcakes," Kim informed him. "Didn't you book us for an upcoming event?"

"Must be for the wedding."

Wedding? She dug her toes into the tips of her shoes and held her breath. "Yours?"

He flashed her a smile. "No. My brother's."

"Of course." She breathed easy once again.

"They've decided to have the ceremony in the new community park."

Kim looked around, confused. "Isn't *this* the new community park?"

Nathaniel's blue eyes sparkled. "The park is two blocks down the street and much larger than my backyard."

"Your *backyard*?"

Kim's mouth popped open in an embarrassed O. Heat seared her cheeks. No wonder he'd been watching her. He was probably wondering what crazy chick was wandering around his property!

And as for the flowers? She doubted he meant them to symbolize anything romantic. Why would he? She was an idiot! The guy was probably just trying to be nice. Or maybe he thought giving her flowers would encourage her to leave. Worse—she would have to face him again in a few weeks at his brother's wedding.

With an inward groan she squeezed her eyes shut, wishing she could start the day over. Or maybe the whole last decade. Then without further ado she set her jaw and looked up.

"Thanks for the roses," she mumbled. And before she could embarrass herself further, she hurried out the gate and back to the cupcake shop—where she belonged.

Acknowledgments

I'D LIKE TO thank my editor at Avon Books, Lucia Macro, for giving me the opportunity to write this book series. It's been a dream come true.

And I'd like to thank my critique partners Jennifer Conner, DV Berkom, Chris Karlsen, and Wanda DeGolier for their inspiration and support.

About the Author

Darlene Panzera writes sweet, fun-loving romance and is a member of the Romance Writers of America's Greater Seattle and Peninsula chapters. Her career launched when her novella *The Bet* was picked by Avon Books and *New York Times* bestselling author Debbie Macomber to be published within Debbie's own novel, *Family Affair*. Darlene says, "I love writing stories that help inspire people to laugh, value relationships, and pursue their dreams."

Born and raised in New Jersey, Darlene is now a resident of the Pacific Northwest, where she lives with her husband and three children. When not writing she enjoys spending time with her family and her two horses and loves camping, hiking, photography, and lazy days at the lake.

Join her on Facebook or at www.darlenepanzera.com.

Visit www.AuthorTracker.com for exclusive information on your favorite HarperCollins authors.

Give in to your impulses . . .
Read on for a sneak peek at five brand-new
e-book original tales of romance
from Avon Books.
Available now wherever e-books are sold.

STEALING HOME
A Diamonds and Dugouts Novel
By Jennifer Seasons

LUCKY LIKE US
Book Two: The Hunted Series
By Jennifer Ryan

STUCK ON YOU
By Cheryl Harper

THE RIGHT BRIDE
Book Three: The Hunted Series
By Jennifer Ryan

LACHLAN'S BRIDE
Highland Lairds Trilogy
By Kathleen Harrington

Raising his glass, Mark smiled and said, "To the rodeo. May you ride your bronc well."

Color tinged Lorelei's cheeks as they tapped their glasses. But her eyes remained on his while he took a long pull of smooth aged whiskey.

Then she spoke, her voice low. "I'll make your head spin, cowboy. That I promise."

That surprised a laugh out of him, even as heat began to pool heavy in his groin. "I'll drink to that." And he did. He lifted the glass and drained it, suddenly anxious to get on to the next stage. A drop of liquid shimmered on her full bottom lip, and it beckoned him. Reaching an arm out, Mark pulled her close and leaned down. With his eyes on hers, he slowly licked the drop off, his tongue teasing her pouty mouth until she released a soft moan.

Arousal coursed through him at the provocative sound.

Pulling her more fully against him, Mark deepened the kiss. Her lush little body fit perfectly against him, and her lips melted under the heat of his. He slid a hand up her back and fisted the dark, thick mass of her long hair. He loved the feel of the cool, silky strands against his skin.

He wanted more.

Tugging gently, Mark encouraged her mouth to open for him. When it did, his tongue slid inside and tasted, explored the exotic flavor of her. Hunger spiked inside him, and he took the kiss deeper. Hotter. She whimpered into his mouth and dug her fingers into his hair, pulled. Her body began pushing against his, restless and searching.

Mark felt like he'd been tossed into an incinerator when he pushed a thigh between her long, shapely legs and discovered the heat there. He groaned and rubbed his thigh against her, feeling her tremble in response.

Suddenly she broke the kiss and pushed out of his arms. Her breathing was ragged, her lips red and swollen from his kiss. Confusion and desire mixed like a heady concoction in his blood, but before he could say anything, she turned and began walking toward the hallway to his bedroom.

At the entrance she stopped and beckoned to him. "Come and get me, catcher."

So she wanted to play, did she? Hell yeah. Games were his life.

Mark toed off his shoes as he yanked his sweater over his head and tossed it on the floor. He began working the button of his fly and strode after her. He was a little unsteady on his feet, but he didn't care. He just wanted to catch her. When he entered his room, he found her by the bed. She'd turned on the bedside lamp, and the light illuminated every gorgeous inch of her curvaceous body.

He started toward her, but she shook her head. "I want you to sit on the bed."

Mark walked to her anyway and gave her a deep, hungry kiss before he sat on the edge of the bed. He wondered what she had in store for him and felt his gut tighten in anticipation. "Are you going to put on a show for me?" *God, it'd be so hot if she did.*

All she said was "mmm hmm." Then she turned her back to him. Mark let his eyes wander over her body and decided her tight, round ass in denim was just about the sexiest thing he'd ever seen.

When his gaze rose back up, he found her smiling over her shoulder at him. "Are you ready for the ride of your life, cowboy?"

Hell yes he was. "Bring it, baby. Show me what you've got."

Her smile grew sultry with unspoken promise as she reached for the hem of her t-shirt. She pulled it up leisurely while she kept eye contact with him. All he could hear was the soft sound of fabric rustling, but it fueled him—this seductively slow striptease she was giving him.

He wanted to see more of her. "Turn around."

As she turned, she continued to pull her shirt up until she was facing him with the yellow cotton dangling loosely from her fingertips. A black, lacy bra barely covered the most voluptuous, gorgeous pair of breasts he'd ever laid eyes on. He couldn't stop staring.

"Do you like what you see?"

Good God, yes. The woman was a goddess. He nodded, a

little harder than he meant to because he almost fell forward. He was starting to tell her how sexy she was when suddenly a full-blown wave of dizziness hit him. He shook his head to clear it. *What the hell?*

"Is everything all right, Mark?"

The room started spinning, and he tried to stand but couldn't. It felt like the world had been tipped sideways and his body was sliding onto the floor. He tried to stand again but fell backward onto the bed instead. He stared up at her as he tried to right himself and couldn't.

Fonda stood there like a siren, dark hair tousled around her head, breasts barely contained—guilt plastered across her stunning face.

Before he fell unconscious on the bed, he knew. Knew it with gut certainty. He tried to tell her, but his mouth wouldn't move. *Son of a bitch.*

Fonda Peters had drugged him.

An Excerpt from

LUCKY LIKE US

Book Two: The Hunted Series

by Jennifer Ryan

The second installment in The Hunted Series
by Jennifer Ryan . . .

1

A wisp of smoke rose from the barrel of his gun. The smell of gunpowder filled the air. Face raised to the night sky, eyes closed, he sucked in a deep breath and let it out slowly, enjoying the moment. Adrenaline coursed through his veins with a thrill that left a tingle in his skin. His heart pounded, and he felt more alive than he remembered feeling ever in his normal life.

Slowly, he lowered his head to the bloody body lying sprawled on the dirty pavement at his feet. The Silver Fox strikes again. The smile spread across his face. He loved the nickname the press had given him after the police spoke of the elusive killer who'd caused at least eight deaths—who knew how many more? He did. He remembered every one of them in minute detail.

He kicked the dead guy in the ribs. Sonofabitch almost ruined everything, but you didn't get to be in his position by leaving the details in a partnership to chance. They'd had a deal, but the idiot had gotten greedy, making him sloppy. He'd set up a meeting for tonight with a new hit but hadn't done the proper background investigation. His death was a direct result of his stupidity.

"You set me up with a cop!" he yelled at the corpse.

He dragged the body by the foot into the steel container, heedless of the man's face scraping across the rough road. He dropped the guy's leg. The loud thud echoed through the cavernous interior. He locked the door and walked through the deserted shipyard, indifferent.

Maybe he'd let his fury get the best of him, but anything, or anyone, who threatened to expose him or end his most enjoyable hobby needed to be eliminated. He had too much to lose, and he never lost.

Only one more loose end to tie up.

2

San Francisco
Thursday, 9:11 p.m.

Little devils stomped up Sam's spine, telling him trouble was on the way. He rolled his shoulders to erase the eerie feeling, but it didn't work, never did. He sensed something was wrong, and he'd learned to trust his instincts. They'd saved his hide more than once.

Sam and his FBI partner, Special Agent Tyler Reed, sat

in their dark car watching the entrance to Ray's Rock House. Every time someone opened the front door, the blare of music poured out into the otherwise quiet street. Sam's contact hadn't arrived yet, but that was what happened when you relied on the less reputable members of society.

"I've got a weird vibe about this," Sam said, breaking the silence. "Watch the front and alley entrances after I go in."

Tyler never took his eyes off the door and the people coming and going. "I've got your back, but I still think we need more agents on this. What's with you lately? Ever since your brother got married and had a family, you've been on edge, taking one dangerous case after another."

Sam remembered the way his brother looked at his wife and the jealousy that had bubbled up in his gut, taking him by surprise. Jenna was everything to Jack, and since they were identical twins, it was easy for Sam to put himself in Jack's shoes. All he had to do was look at Jack, Jenna, and their two boys to see what it would be like if he found someone to share his life.

Sam had helped Jenna get rid of her abusive ex-husband, who'd kidnapped her a couple years before. Until Jack had come into her life, she'd been alone, hiding from her ex— simply existing, she'd said. Very much like him.

An Excerpt from

STUCK ON YOU

by Cheryl Harper

Love's in the limelight when big-shot producer
KT Masters accidentally picks a fight with
Laura Charles, a single mother working as
a showgirl waitress in a hotel bar. When he
offers her the fling of a lifetime, Laura's willing
to play along . . . just so long as her heart
stays out of it. If she can help it, that is!

Laura said, "Excuse me, Mr. Masters." When he held up an impatient hand, she narrowed her eyes and turned back to the two women. "Maybe you can tell him the drinks are here? I've got other customers to take care of."

The pink-haired woman held out a hand. "Sure thing. I'm Mandy, the makeup artist. This is Shane. She'll do hair. We'll both help with costumes and props as needed."

As Laura shook their hands, she privately thought that might be the best arrangement. Shane's hair was perfect, not one strand out of place. Mandy's pink shag sort of made it look like she'd been caught in a windstorm. In a convertible. But her makeup and clothes were very cute.

KT said, "Hold on just a sec, Bob. Let me go ahead and tweet this. Gotta keep the fans interested, you know."

Laura glanced over her bare shoulder to see KT bound down the stairs, pause, snap a picture, and then type something on his phone before shouting about taking down the electronic display in the corner. Lucky would not be happy about that. As KT waved his arms dramatically and the director nodded, Laura smiled at the two girls. "Guess I'm dismissed."

They laughed, and Laura turned to skirt their table as she reached for the drink tray. Being unable to move, like her feathers had attached themselves to the floor, was her first clue that something had gone horribly wrong. And when KT Masters bumped into her, sending the tray skidding into the sodas she'd just delivered, she knew exactly who was responsible. She tried to whirl around to give him a piece of her mind but spun in place and then heard a loud rip just before she bumped into the table and sent two glasses crashing to the floor. She might have followed them, but KT wrapped a hand around her arm to steady her. His warm skin was a brand against her chilly flesh.

The only sound in Viva Las Vegas was the tinny *plink* of electricity through one million bright white bulbs. Every eye was focused on the drama taking place at the foot of the stage. Before she could really get a firm grip on the embarrassment, irritation, shock, and downright anger boiling over, Laura shouted, "You ripped off my feather!"

Even the light bulbs seemed to hold their breath at that point.

KT's hand slid down her arm, raising goose bumps as it went, before he slammed both hands on his hips, and Laura shivered. The heat from that one hand made her wonder what it would be like to be pressed up against him. Instead of the flannel robe, she should put a KT Masters on her birthday list. She wouldn't have to worry about being cold ever again.

"Yeah, I did you a favor. This costume has real potential"—he motioned with one hand as he looked her over from collarbone to knee—"but the feathers get in the way, so . . . you're welcome!" The frown looked all wrong on his face, like he didn't have a lot of experience with anger or irritation, but the look in his eyes was as warm as his hand had been. When he rubbed his palms together, she thought maybe she wasn't the only one to be surprised by the heat.

They both looked down at the bedraggled pink feather, now swimming in ice cubes and spilled soda under his left shoe. No matter how much she hated the feathers or how valid his point about their ridiculousness was, she wasn't going to let him get away with this. He should apologize. Any decent person would.

"What are you going to do about it?" She plopped her hands on her own hips, thrust her chin out, and met his angry stare.

He straightened and flashed a grim smile before leaning down to scrape the feather up off the floor. He pinched the driest edge and held it out from his body. "Never heard 'the customer's always right,' have you?"

Laura snatched the feather away. "In what way are you a customer? I only see a too-important big shot who can't apologize."

His opened his mouth to say . . . something, then changed his mind and pointed a finger in her face instead. "Oh, really? I bet if I went to have a little talk with the manager or Miss

An Excerpt from

THE RIGHT BRIDE

BOOK THREE: THE HUNTED SERIES

by Jennifer Ryan

The Hunted Series continues with this
third installment by Jennifer Ryan . . .

1

Shelly swiped the lip gloss wand across her lips, rolled them in and out to smooth out the color, and grinned at herself in the mirror, satisfied with the results. She pushed up her boobs, exposing just enough flesh to draw a man's attention, and keep it, but still not look too obvious.

"Perfect. He'll love it."

Ah, Cameron Shaw. Rich and powerful, sexy as hell, and kind in a way that made it easy to get what she wanted. Exactly the kind of husband she'd always dreamed about marrying.

Shelly had grown up in a nice middle class family. Ordinary. She desperately wanted to be anything but ordinary.

She'd grown up a plump youngster and a fat teenager. At fifteen, she'd resorted to binging and purging and starved herself thin. Skinny and beautiful—boys took notice. You can get a guy to do just about anything when you offer them hot sex. By the time she graduated high school, she'd transformed herself into the most popular girl in the place.

For Shelly, destined to live a glamorous life in a big house with servants and fancy cars and clothes, meeting Cameron in the restaurant had been a coup.

Executives and wealthy businessmen frequented the upscale restaurant. She'd gone fishing and landed her perfect catch. Now, she needed to hold on and reel in a marriage proposal.

2

Night fell outside Cameron's thirty-sixth-floor office window. Tired, he'd spent all day in meetings. For the president of Merrick International, long hours were the norm and sleepless nights were a frequent occurrence.

The sky darkened and beckoned the stars to come to life. If he were out on the water, and away from the glow of the city lights, he'd see them better, twinkling in all their brilliant glory.

He couldn't remember the last time he'd taken out the sailboat. He'd promised Emma he'd take her fishing. Every time he planned to go, something came up at work. More and more often, he put her off in favor of some deal or problem that couldn't wait. He needed to realign his priorities. His daughter deserved better.

He stared at the picture of his golden girl. Emma was five now and the image of her mother: long, wavy golden hair and deep blue eyes. She always looked at him with such love. He remembered Caroline looking at him the same way.

They'd been so happy when they discovered Caroline was pregnant. In the beginning, things had been so sweet. They'd lain awake at night talking about whether it would be a boy or a girl, what they'd name their child, and what they thought he or she would grow up to be.

He never thought he'd watch his daughter grow up without Caroline beside him.

The pregnancy took a turn in the sixth month when Caroline began having contractions. They gave her medication to stop them and put her on bed rest for the rest of the pregnancy.

One night he'd come home to find her pale and hurting. He rushed her to the hospital. Her blood pressure spiked, and the contractions started again. No amount of medication could stop them. Two hours later, when the contractions were really bad, the doctor came in to tell him Caroline's body was failing. Her liver and kidneys were shutting down.

Caroline was a wreck. He still heard her pleading for him to save the baby. She delivered their daughter six weeks early, then suffered a massive stroke and died without ever holding her child.

Cameron picked up the photograph and traced his daughter's face, the past haunting his thoughts. He'd spent three weeks in the Neonatal Intensive Care Unit, grieving for his wife and begging his daughter to live. Week four had been a turning point. He felt she'd spent three weeks mourning the loss of her mother and then decided to live for her father. She began eating on her own and gained weight quickly. Ten days

An Excerpt from

LACHLAN'S BRIDE
HIGHLAND LAIRDS TRILOGY
by Kathleen Harrington

Lady Francine Walsingham can't believe
Lachlan MacRath, laird and pirate, is to be her
escort into Scotland. But trust him she must, for
Francine has no choice but to act as his lover to
keep her enemies at bay. When Lachlan first sees
Francine, the English beauty stirs his blood like
no woman has ever before. And now that they
must play the besotted couple so he can protect
her, Lachlan is determined to use all his seductive
prowess to properly woo her into his bed.

May 1496
The Cheviot Hills
The Border Between England and Scotland

Stretched flat on the blood-soaked ground, Lachlan Mac-Rath gazed up at the cloudless morning sky and listened to the exhausted moans of the wounded.

The dead and the dying lay scattered across the lush spring grass. Overhead, the faint rays of dawn broke above the hilltops as the buttercups and bluebells dipped and swayed in the soft breeze. The gruesome corpses were sprawled amidst the wildflowers, their vacant eyes staring upward to the heavens, the stumps of their severed arms and legs still oozing blood and gore. Dented helmets, broken swords, axes, and pikes gave mute testimony to the ferocity of the combatants. Here and there, a loyal destrier, trained to war, grazed calmly alongside its fallen master.

Following close upon daylight, the scavengers would come

creeping, ready to strip the bodies of anything worth a shilling: armor, dirks, boots, belts. If they were Scotsmen, he'd be in luck. If not, he'd soon be dead. There wasn't a blessed thing he could do but wait. He was pinned beneath his dead horse, and all efforts to free himself during the night had proven fruitless.

In the fierce battle of the evening before, the warriors on horseback had left behind all who'd fallen. Galloping across the open, rolling countryside, Scots and English had fought savagely, until it was too dark to tell friend from foe. There was no way of knowing the outcome of the battle, for victory had been determined miles away.

Hell, it was Lachlan's own damn fault. He'd come on the foray into England with King James for a lark. After delivering four new cannons to the castle at Roxburgh, along with the Flemish master gunners to fire them, he'd decided not to return to his ship immediately as planned. The uneventful crossing on the *Sea Hawk* from the Low Countries to Edinburgh, followed by the tedious journey to the fortress, with the big guns pulled by teams of oxen, had left him eager for a bit of adventure.

When he'd learned that the king was leading a small force into Northumberland to retrieve cattle raided by Sassenach outlaws, the temptation to join them had been too great to resist. There was nothing like a hand-to-hand skirmish with his ancient foe to get a man's blood pumping through his veins.

But Lord Dacre, Warden of the Marches, had surprised the Scots with a much larger, well-armed force of his own, and what should have been a carefree rout had turned into deadly combat.

A plea for help interrupted Lachlan's brooding thoughts.

Not far away, a wounded English soldier who'd cried out in pain during the night raised himself up on one elbow.

"Lychester! Over here, sir! It's Will Jeffries!"

Lachlan watched from beneath slit lids as another Sassenach came into view. Attired in the splendid armor of the nobility, the newcomer rode a large, caparisoned black horse. He'd clearly come looking for someone, for he held the reins of a smaller chestnut, its saddle empty and waiting.

"Here I am, Marquess," the young man named Jeffries called weakly. He lifted one hand in a trembling wave as the Marquess of Lychester drew near to his countryman. Dismounting, he approached the wounded soldier.

"Thank God," Jeffries said with a hoarse groan. "I've taken a sword blade in my thigh. The cut's been oozing steadily. I was afraid I wouldn't make it through the night."

Lychester didn't say a word. He came to stand behind the injured man, knelt down on one knee, and raised his fallen comrade to a seated position. Grabbing a hank of the man's yellow hair, the marquess jerked the fair head back and deftly slashed the exposed throat from ear to ear. Then he calmly wiped his blade on the youth's doublet, lifted him up in his arms, and threw the body facedown over the chestnut's back.

The English nobleman glanced around, checking, no doubt, to see if there'd been a witness to the coldblooded execution. Lachlan held his breath and remained motionless, his lids still lowered over his eyes. Apparently satisfied, the marquess mounted, grabbed the reins of the second horse, and rode away.

Lachlan slowly exhaled.

Sonofabitch.